D1748634

HEAVEN'S HOPE

THE EDWARDS BROTHERS SERIES
BOOK 3

Heaven's Hope

The Edwards Brothers Series
Book 3

KIKI CHALUPNIK

Xulon Press Elite

Xulon Press Elite
2301 Lucien Way #415
Maitland, FL 32751
407.339.4217
www.xulonpress.com

Exulon
ELITE

© 2021 by Kiki Chalupnik

All rights reserved solely by the author. The author guarantees all contents are original and do not infringe upon the legal rights of any other person or work. No part of this book may be reproduced in any form without the permission of the author. The views expressed in this book are not necessarily those of the publisher.

Unless otherwise indicated, Scripture quotations taken from the Holy Bible, New International Version (NIV). Copyright © 1973, 1978, 1984, 2011 by Biblica, Inc.™. Used by permission. All rights reserved.

Scripture quotations taken from the New King James Version (NKJV). Copyright © 1982 by Thomas Nelson, Inc. Used by permission. All rights reserved.

<a href="https://www.vectorstock.com/royalty-free-vector/bouquet-flowers-line-art-tropialdecorative-vector-31101914">Vector image by VectorStock / vectorstock</a>

This is a work of fiction. All of the characters, names, incidents, organizations, and dialogue, in this novel are either products of the author's imagination or are used fictitiously.

Printed in the United States of America.

ISBN-13: 978-1-6628-1137-1

Table of Contents

Acknowledgements vii
In Memorium ix

Chapter 1 1
Chapter 2 3
Chapter 3 7
Chapter 4 11
Chapter 5 17
Chapter 6 25
Chapter 7 31
Chapter 8 33
Chapter 9 41
Chapter 10 55
Chapter 11 71
Chapter 12 77
Chapter 13 83
Chapter 14 89
Chapter 15 99
Chapter 16 111
Chapter 17 117
Chapter 18 125
Chapter 19 131
Chapter 20 141
Chapter 21 145
Chapter 22 149
Chapter 23 153
Chapter 24 157

ACKNOWLEDGEMENTS

To all my readers:

Thank you for all your kind words and encouragement; they have meant so much to me. It gives me great pleasure to know you have enjoyed reading my books. I know several of you have been anxiously waiting for Book 3 in the Edwards' Brothers Series. Here it is. Happy Reading!

A special thanks to friends who have always been more than willing to read my manuscript. Thanks for your positive input, corrections, and suggestions to rewrite any confusing thoughts.

My faithful readers are Di Rasmusson, Elaine Sola, and Linda Van Noy. A special thanks to Libby LaLond, an editor by profession who graciously volunteered to read my manuscript, Heaven's Hope. I am so grateful to each of you. I know you have sacrificed much of your time.

Thank you to Bridgett and the editorial staff at Xulon Press. They have been a pleasure to work with.

There are no words to express my love and gratefulness to my family. Our children, Rick and his wife, Sue; Janet and her husband, Mike. They have always been such an encouragement and have given us great joy in who they are and what God has done in each of their lives. To our four adult grandchildren Kali, and the three T's (Tyler, Trevor, and Travis)—Papa and I are so proud of you. You bless us every day. I love you more, but God loves you most.

My best friend of 59 years, my husband, Rick, has been the love of my life, protector, and godly example of what a husband should be. We love strong and laugh much. Thank you for your fierce and faithful love all these years.

My prayer is that my stories express my heart and encourage the reader to know God and His great love for each of us. To Him be the glory.

Psalm 115:1 (NIV)

Not to us, Lord, not to us
but to your name be the glory,
because of your love and faithfulness.

IN MEMORIUM

This book is dedicated to my dear friend, Dorothy Carlson, who went to be with her Lord and Savior one year before Heaven's Hope was completed. Dorothy was first my high school Sunday school teacher and youth leader. As time went on, she and her husband, Al, became two of our dearest friends. This friendship continued for well over 50 years. Although separated by distance, we were never separated by our hearts. Dorothy encouraged me in my writing and always looked forward to reading each of my books. She and Al are greatly missed by many.

Chapter 1

> Many waters cannot quench love,
> Nor can the floods drown it.
> If a man would give for love
> All the wealth of his house,
> It would be utterly despised.
>
> —*Song of Solomon 8:7 (NKJV)*

Mark Hamilton had never prayed so hard in his life ... at least not for himself. He desperately needed wisdom and discernment for the decision he was about to make. He knew he loved her from the day she walked into the law office of Fletcher, Hoffman, and Jackson, however, so much of his life had been on hold for a long time.

Mark was seventeen and Jessie, his sister, only thirteen, when their dad had passed away suddenly from an aneurism. This left his mom, sister, and himself devastated beyond words. Mark had always looked up to his dad and hoped to one day be even half the man he was. With the sudden loss of their father, Mark instantly became the man of the house—dad to Jessie, and someone his mother completely depended on. Their world, as they knew it, was turned upside down. Mark became an amazing role model for his sister and kept tight reins on her studies and extracurricular activities. Right after high school, he enrolled in the local community college, so he would remain close to home. When Jessie graduated from high school, Mark went on to law school. He remained close to his mom and sister and would go home as often as possible. His mom had become a strong, independent woman over the years. She now lived in a 55 plus community in Florida.

After graduating from law school, Mark was immediately hired by the Texas law firm he had completed an internship with. Making partner four years ago was a tremendous blessing. It afforded him the freedom and opportunity to care for his sister, Jessie, when she experienced a horrible crisis in her life. First, the loss of her military husband, Jake, and then a horrific accident where she lost her memory for over a month. He and his mom shared the anguish of their missing daughter and sister for over a month. Now, she was happily married to an amazing man. Jason Edwards was the man who had rescued her from this horrible accident. Jason and Jessie had been married for two years now and had a beautiful baby girl, Anna Beth. His sister also had a boy, Jake, from her first marriage and a nephew, who Mark had loved as his own from the time he was born. Little Jake's dad died in Iraq never knowing his son. At the time, it was difficult for his sister to go on—he knew that with God's strength and grace, however, she would be able to cope with her loss. And she did.

Chapter 2

Mark believed in his heart that now was his time. He had always wanted a wife and family. However, he had put his own desires on hold until he knew his sister and mom were good without him. The only problem—the woman he had fallen in love with five years ago had married his best friend, Dan. Lacey McPherson had been with the law firm almost as long as he had. When Mr. Hoffman retired from the firm, four years ago, Mark was given the opportunity to make senior partner, an invitation he could not refuse. The title for the company now was, Fletcher, Jackson, and Hamilton, Attorneys at Law. Mark handled the corporate side of the firm. He was a man of integrity and strong faith and Mark credited his promotion to God's blessing.

Now he was faced with the hardest decision of his life. Marry the woman he was in love with or find another.

Mark and Dan had been close all through law school. In fact, their friendship began while roommates in college. Dan was a handsome, fun-loving guy. Although not as tall as Mark, Dan was a good six feet with black hair and blue eyes, and the girls loved him. He could make anyone laugh. His only problem in college; he liked to party. He called Mark an old fuddy-duddy because he never wanted to join him. He went with him a couple of times to prove that he wasn't such a fuddy-duddy, however, partying was never something he really enjoyed. Mark found a church as soon as he started college and a Bible study that he was committed to. Often, Mark would invite Dan to join him, but Dan always declined. It was not uncommon that Dan had been out most of the night and only wanted to sleep. Mark was patient and loved Dan as he would a brother.

Mark excelled in every way. He spent many hours tutoring his friend so he could pass the bar exam. He had to take it twice, but Mark was such an encourager that when Dan wanted to throw in the towel, it was Mark who spurred him on. Mark knew the pressure his buddy was under. It wasn't just normal pressure; it was relentless. Dan's father was a judge and his mother a prosecuting attorney. Mark had spent many a night at their dinner table. He wasn't sure if they even liked him, but they always compared Dan to him, embarrassing both of them. They had been such tight friends that Mark had been Dan's best man at he and Lacey's wedding. There was never a doubt in Mark's mind that if Lacey and Dan were still married, he would have continued to keep his feelings for Lacey hidden. But Dan had been killed in a rock-climbing accident two months ago.

Mark was first to be hired on at Fletcher, Hoffman, and Jackson. Six months later, Dan was hired on with the same firm. Although Dan was not offered the position of partner, he was content being an associate. Dan totally understood that Mark was more qualified than he. Mark remembered all too well the last conversation he had with his friend before his untimely death. Dan stepped into Mark's office that Friday morning with the biggest grin on his face.

"Hey, what's up buddy?" Dan could hardly control himself as he shared with his friend that he and Lacey were pregnant. Mark sat with his mouth agape—then congratulated him with the biggest bear hug.

"I'm truly happy for you and Lacey; that's great!" He had to admit, it felt like a knife had been plunged into his heart.

CHAPTER 2

Dan tried convincing Mark to go climbing with him the following day, which was a Saturday. "I'm probably not going to get too many more chances to climb, and once the baby comes, it will be slim to none."

"Thanks for the offer, but no way," said Mark. "I want my feet firmly planted on good old terra firma."

For some reason this ignited a burning question in Mark's soul. "Buddy, if you died on that mountain tomorrow, do you know where you would spend eternity?" Mark would never forget the distant look in his best friend's eyes.

It seemed like an eternity as Dan searched his face before answering, "No, Mark, I honestly can't say that I know. But the one thing I do know—I want what you have." He said he wanted the peace and joy that he knew his friend had. Mark shared the Gospel with him, as he had many times before. Evidently Dan's heart was never ready to make the most important decision of his life. But at that time, Dan was ready, and he knew what he needed to do.

All these years Mark had prayed for his friend, still his reply nearly blew him away. As they stood in Mark's office, it was only moments before the two friends were on their knees praying. Dan asked God to forgive him his sins and come into his heart. Mark gave his friend the Bible he kept in his desk drawer before Dan walked out of his office. That was the last time he saw his best friend alive. He wiped the tears that had started to escape. He knew without a doubt he would see his friend once again ... but it was tough, very tough.

Chapter 3

Lacey Cramson collapsed on the floor after reading a letter from her father-in-law. She was sure her pain and moaning were heard to the ends of the earth. She trembled and shook in fear. *How could these people even be human?* her heart cried. In her wildest dream, or nightmare, she would never have imagined anyone could be so cruel. Lacey was just over three months pregnant. She needed to protect her baby, but what could she do? She wished they had never told Dan's parents of her pregnancy.

Lacey did the only thing she could think of. She sat in the leather chair in front of her husband's best friend. Mark read through the letter Lacey brought to him. His heart went out to her as she sat with red puffy eyes. The sparkle was gone from her eyes; replaced with a sad, hollow glaze. He wanted to wrap her in his arms. "Mark, what am I to do?"

Mark read the sentence that Judge Cramson repeated several times. *Dan's mother and I cannot allow our grandchild to be raised by a single parent.* Mark looked into Lacey's eyes, "Well, it certainly looks like this is their biggest concern—at least that is what they are making it out to be. They know that you will be a single mother raising their grandchild." Mark saw the sadness in Lacey's eyes as she agreed with him.

"Mark, what can I do? Can I fight them?"

"Lacey, it will be difficult mainly because of who they are. You will be going up against a superior court judge and a prosecuting attorney. Two people with connections in high places. Even if we found an attorney willing to take the case, you know they are going to fight it. I don't know what kind of money Dan left you, but knowing my friend, I expect he left you well taken care of."

Lacey held back a strained laugh. "Dan left me almost penniless, Mark. Oh, I know this was not his intention at all. I got the house—with a mortgage, and an insurance policy worth twenty-five-thousand."

"What? I find that hard to believe, Lacey. He always talked about taking care of you. I'm sure with a baby on the way he wanted to make sure you would be set."

"Yes, I would be set if he had transferred the beneficiary on a two-million-dollar policy."

Mark looked at Lacey in utter confusion. "What do you mean if he had transferred the beneficiary on a policy? Are you sure he hadn't done that?"

"I'm positive. It was a policy his parents took out on him before we married. He had asked his parents to take care of it. They never did."

"So, you're saying they cashed in on the policy and got the two million?"

"Yes, I'm sure they did." Mark shook his head in disbelief. "Mark, you know they never liked me. I did not fit their expectations for their son. I certainly didn't come from their circle of celebrities or the elite crowd. I worked here as nothing more than a glorified receptionist. They never understood what Dan saw in me."

"Hey, don't put yourself down. Everyone here loved you." *I know that I have always loved you from the first day I laid eyes on you.*

"Well, I'm not here now. Mark, I don't even have a job." The tears began to flow once again. She told him that Dan wanted Lacey to quit her job soon after they found out they were pregnant. Mark handed her a tissue that he took from the box on the side table next to his desk.

CHAPTER 3

"We should never have been so quick to tell Dan's parents I was pregnant. I'll never forget the look on their faces when Dan told them—shock, disdain, anger. Whatever, they were not pleased as most grandparents would be. In fact, they looked at their son and said, '"What in the world were you thinking?"' "Can you imagine how I felt at that moment?" The tears poured from her eyes and Mark's heart broke a little more.

"Lacey, I am so sorry. May I keep this letter? I would like to see what we can do."

"Of course. I appreciate anything, anything at all, Mark." Lacey got up from her chair and gave Mark a look he had never seen on anyone's face—red swollen eyes, sadness, utter defeat. He knew how badly she had to be hurting. He wanted to enfold her in an embrace that would comfort and protect her, but he knew he couldn't so he settled for a quick casual hug. The same kind of hug he would give his sister. He would never betray his friend. He simply walked her to the door and said he would be praying for her. She nodded as she walked out the door.

Chapter 4

"Mark, do you have any idea what you are saying?" Mark was seated on the back patio of his sister Jessie's home. Her husband, Jason, had built them a beautiful home in an exclusive suburb of New York City. Mark loved visiting as often as possible. He loved his nephew, Jake, and his niece, Anna Beth. He had finished explaining Lacey's situation and his solution to her dilemma.

"All I know is that I love her, Jess. I have loved her for over five years."

"Why did you wait until now to do something about it?"

"I don't want you to feel guilty, Jess, but I honestly felt you and mom were my priority. There was no way I was going to contemplate any personal feelings I was having for someone, especially a woman I had just met and worked with."

"Oh, Mark, I'm so sorry. You gave up a lot for mom and me." Her eyes began to glisten with unshed tears. "What you're saying now is that you think you should marry her." He slowly nodded as she put the letter down that he had given her to read; the one from Dan's father. "This letter is filled with disdain and venom for his daughter-in-law. How can anyone treat another human being like that?"

"Yeah, I know. My heart was breaking in two for her, Jess. As I read and re-read this letter, or threat, I spent the whole night in prayer. It was like God kept telling me to do this. I don't know why, but I'm convinced this is what God wants from me."

"First of all, Mark, is she a Christian?"

"She's as Christian as most people in the U.S. A good person, and if God had a scale, her good would certainly outweigh the bad in her life. Isn't that what a lot of people think?"

"You're so right. But what are you going to do about being unequally yoked? You always reminded me of this."

"I know. It's totally what the Bible teaches." Mark ran his fingers through his hair and rubbed his face. Looking at his sister, he said, "Jess, if I only marry her to give her baby a name and a reason for Dan's parents to see that she won't be a single parent, maybe we can still be a family."

"Oh Mark, how can you sacrifice so much for someone that doesn't love you?"

"But I love her, Jess. I'm willing to love her and protect her as long as she will let me."

Just then, Jason came walking through the patio door to join them. "Hey Mark, good to see you. What brings you all the way to New York? Too hot in Texas for you?"

"I wish that was the reason." Jessie began to explain the situation to her husband. Jason sat motionless as he heard the heartache Lacey was going through. He looked over at his brother-in-law. "I know what you're thinking—how can I love someone who I know may never love me back? Am I right?"

"Yeah, that's pretty much it." Mark excused himself to run to the rest room. "I'll be right back."

When he was gone, Jason turned to his beautiful wife. "Honey, do you know what I see in all of this?" Jessie looked quizzically at her husband and shook her head. "I see a picture of God's love for us. What does that verse say in 1 John? This is love: not that we loved God, but that he loved us. I see this as a perfect picture of God's sacrifice for us. He loves us no matter what, whether we love him in return or not. He waits patiently for us. I know he was certainly patient in waiting for me to love him. It's obvious that Mark loves Lacey so much and is willing to wait for her to one day return that love."

CHAPTER 4

Jessie had to agree with her husband. "Jason, I never looked at it that way, and knowing my brother, he would never want his love for Lacey compared to God's love for us—babe, you are so right. It just sounds so drastic. I can't imagine loving you as much as I do, and then to think that you could never love me back would break my heart." Jessie reached for her husband's hand, drawing it to her lips.

Mark returned and took a chair next to his brother-in-law. Jason looked at Mark with eyes heavy with question. "You're actually willing to marry Dan's wife? What about her love for her husband?"

"For one thing, I could never betray Dan. I know he loved her, and she loved him. I know she still loves him."

"Have you talked to Lacey about this?" continued Jason. "Maybe she would have a strong objection to your proposal."

"She might. I don't know. No, I haven't mentioned it to her. She was in my office on Thursday. I spent all of Thursday night praying and seeking God's direction. Friday morning, I was convinced that this is what God would want me to do. I couldn't bear to see her lose her and Dan's child."

"Do you really believe Judge Cramson, that's his name, right?" Jason asked with such concern in his eyes. Mark nodded his response. "You believe he would do such a cruel thing?"

"I really believe he can and would do this. Like I said, he knows a lot of people." Mark told them of her financial predicament and the deceptive way her in-laws had never changed Dan's life insurance policy."

Jessie couldn't keep quiet. "Oh man, they're a couple of rats. How could they do this to Lacey and their grandchild? Mark, you need to tell Mom about your plans."

"Yes, I know. But I think I'll wait until I have talked to Lacey. She may not want anything to do with such a hairbrained idea, or even me for that matter. All I ask is for you guys to really pray about it. Right now, I have peace that this is the right thing to do. I may feel differently about this plan by the time I get off the plane."

"But Mark," Jessie could not help but ask the question, "what if she never loves you back. How long will you wait?"

"I'll wait as long as it takes."

"And what if she wants out of the marriage after a few years ... what then?" asked Jason.

"All I can say is that I'll have to let her go. I won't force myself on her ... in any way. I know it would be hard, but I'll let her go if that's what she wants." Jessie and Jason sat in disbelief. Jessie always knew she had an exceptional brother and now her husband knew as well.

"So, how long will you be staying?" His sister was anxious to have him spend a few days with the family.

"I was going to leave tomorrow night, but I can stay until Sunday night if I can get a flight. I really need to be in the office Monday."

Jason jumped in without hesitation. "Hey, stay until Sunday night. You can take the company jet. No reservation required."

"Thanks, man. Maybe the extra time will give me a chance to sort all this out in my head—and my heart."

The baby monitor went off and Jason and Jessie looked at one another. "Your turn or mine?" asked Jason.

"Whose turn is it usually?" Jessie gave him a playful swat on his arm as she stood to go get their six-month-old daughter, Anna Beth.

Jason turned to his brother-in-law. "Mark, I have to be perfectly honest with you. You know when Jessie had her amnesia and could not remember her late husband, Jake? Well, once she gained her memory, I had a really hard time and wondered if she was still in love with him. I knew he was gone but I had a difficult time thinking about her not being able to really love me. I knew I couldn't compete with a dead husband. I know this has to be tough, but how do you feel about something like that?"

"Yeah, I hear you. All I can say is that you never knew Jess's husband, Jake. Dan had been my best friend for a long time. We were in law school together. In fact, we had been friends since the last two years in college—our friendship just clicked. I would do anything for him. I feel if

CHAPTER 4

God wants me to do this, I want to be obedient to his will and purpose. Who knows, she may not want any part of my proposal. I can only try."

"Uncle Mark! Uncle Mark!" Mark turned as Jake came running out onto the patio jumping up into his uncle's arms. Jake was an adorable three-and-a-half-year-old little boy who had always adored his uncle Mark.

"Hey buddy, what have you been up to? I missed you."

"I was sleeping. Mommy said I was crankly and need a nap." The two men stifled a laugh at his pronunciation of cranky.

He slid off his uncle's lap and ran into the arms of his dad. Mark knew that Jason loved this little guy as if he were his biological father; never a doubt in any of their minds of the love he had for him. *Could it possibly be the same for me if I raised Dan and Lacey's child? That would be up to Lacey. I know I could love him like my own.* He had a lot of questions that would have to be answered.

"Daddy, there's Momma and Anna Beth!" He pointed to Jessie as she came out to join them. "Uncle Mark, Daddy said I can play wiff my sister when she can walk. Right Daddy?"

"That's right, my little man. And right now, you can only sit and hold her in your lap, right?" He nodded his head in total agreement.

"And I'm gonna be her potector when I get bigger, right Daddy?"

"Yep, you will be the best big brother and protector any sister could have."

Mark was enjoying the interaction between his nephew and his brother-in-law. He looked over at his sister and saw such pride and joy in her eyes. She walked over to her brother and settled Anna Beth in his arms.

"Who knows, Mark, you might be a dad before you know it."

Mark's heart constricted at that thought. If that's what God wanted, he would be open to being the father Lacey's child would need. *Would Lacey even agree to him being the father?*

Chapter 5

Mark flew out Sunday night on the Edwards' private plane. It certainly gave him more time to spend with his sister and her family. He was grateful for the time they had to pray together before he left. The flight from New York to Dallas gave him time to read his Bible and pray some more. He needed God's wisdom and discernment; the more he read and prayed, the more convinced he was that this was what God wanted him to do—but would Lacey agree?

Monday morning Mark had several briefs he needed to go over. By the afternoon he knew he had to call Lacey to set up a time when they could meet. He had no idea what her weekend had to be like. He probably should have called to let her know he was flying to New York, but it was a last-minute decision he made. She had no idea how much prayer he had given to this—Jess and Jason were also praying for her. He thought her decision was much greater than his. He already knew he loved her.

Lacey's voice sounded so sad and lost when she answered the phone. He couldn't imagine the broken heart she must have—first the loss of Dan, now her in-laws and their demands.

"Lacey, it's Mark. How are you holding up?"

"Not too well, Mark. I got another threatening letter from Judge Cramson. This one worse than the first. He's insisting I sign a document promising to give them my baby when he or she is born."

"Lacey, are you free to talk tonight? I think I have a solution to this preposterous situation. I can make it to your house around seven—would that work for you?"

"Yes, that's fine. Mark, I can't imagine that there's any solution to this. It's just horrible. I can't eat. I can't sleep. I'm a wreck."

Mark arrived at Lacey's home only to find her with red swollen eyes and looking gaunt. He wanted to wrap her in his arms and hold her tight. While she may have welcomed it, he wasn't about to take that chance. He led her to the living room and Mark took a seat on the couch. Lacey handed him the most recent letter and document she had received from Dan's father. As he read, to his dismay, it all looked legitimate—they really wanted Dan's baby. *I may as well jump right in and get this over with.*

"Lacey, I first want you to know that I have done a lot of praying about this proposal I have for you. The decision is entirely up to you." Man, he was nervous. His hands were sweaty—he was sure sweat was beading on his brow. *Why would I be so nervous if God is in this?* But then he heard a voice saying, *trust me, Mark, just trust me*. "Lacey, I want to marry you. Don't get me wrong, I know you loved Dan and still do…" he took another deep breath. "I believe if we marry, the Cramsons will have nothing to fight with." Mark looked at Lacey as she sat wringing her hands and biting her lower lip. "Lacey, did you hear me?"

"Yes, I heard you, Mark. But why would you even suggest this? I don't understand why you would want to do such a thing."

"Like I said, it's up to you. If we were married, you would not be a single mom. I would be there to help raise Dan's and your child. I know you loved Dan and I don't want to take that away from you at all. We could call it a marriage of convenience. I don't expect any other arrangement. I just know I want to be there for you and your baby. You can take your time and think about it."

Lacey burst into tears and Mark, not thinking, wrapped her in a gentle embrace. He sat holding her as they sat together on the couch. "I know this is a lot to take in, but I want you to know that this is something

CHAPTER 5

I want to do for you, and for Dan. So, think about it." He would have told her to pray about it, however, he didn't know what her relationship to God was like. He realized that didn't matter, so he added, "and pray about it."

She looked up at him with her amazing green eyes that were so sad and doe-like. She immediately lowered her head as if embarrassed to look at him. He unconsciously brushed her hair away from her face. *She's beautiful even if she is a mess.* He was always mesmerized by her cinnamon-colored hair and stunning green eyes; after all, she was a McPherson. Her hair was always in a chignon or a loose twist. He had wondered what it would look like not being so formal. "Lacey, look at me." He held her shoulders and gently asked again for her to look up at him. As she obeyed, Mark told her that everything would be okay. "You need to trust me in this, Lace."

"Mark, I don't need any time to think about it. I just don't understand why you would sacrifice so much for me." His heart longed to tell her how he had always loved her, but he held back. He knew she had to still love Dan; he hadn't been gone that long at all. She was grieving for her husband.

"I want to do this. I believe God is telling me to do this. Lacey, there is something else that I think we need to consider, and this may very well be the hardest decision for you to make." She looked at him and gave a nod. "When the baby is born, I think you should put me down as the father. This way the Cramsons will not have any rights unless they demand a DNA test. I seriously doubt they would do that. They weren't the greatest parents to Dan from what I knew of them. And, after how they treated his stepbrother, I have no idea."

"Stepbrother? I didn't even know he had a stepbrother."

"Yeah, he has a stepbrother that I believe is about five or six years older than him."

"He never told me. That's very strange. I don't think he was even at our wedding."

"I never really knew him, but he always was kind of strange when he showed up for family dinners. It was obvious his mother, or I should say step-mother, always put him down. But his dad favored him over Dan. They were really a dysfunctional family to say the least.

"Getting back to our conversation, what do you think of my proposal? I'm willing if you are."

"Okay. I hate to think of what you are giving up for me. It's definitely a solution I never expected to hear. I guess I'm willing if you are. As for listing you as the father—I don't want to betray Dan."

"I understand, Lacey. I certainly do not want you to do that."

"I wish I could say that I would love you as you should be loved, because you deserve to be loved as a wife loves her husband—but right now, Mark, I can't promise that either."

"I'm not expecting you to love me as a wife loves her husband. As far as Dan's child, you and I both know he will always be the biological father of that new life you are carrying, and I will never take that away from you or Dan. The baby will grow up knowing that as far as I'm concerned."

"Well, when do you want to get married?" He could tell there was some trepidation in her question.

"Whenever you're ready. We need to make sure that the Cramsons are well aware of us marrying. I will have the papers drawn up with your response to his letters. I guess the next question is, where do you want to live? I have a two-bedroom condo in downtown Dallas, but I think we should live in your house. There is more room for you and the baby here."

"Mark, you're already sacrificing so much, and now you're willing to give up your home for me? Your condo is close to your office; I live in Arlington. You would have a commute every day to downtown Dallas."

"It'll work. I won't mind the commute at all. Arlington is only 21 miles from Dallas, maybe an extra five miles to your house but that's not a bad commute at all. I'll sell my condo; I'm sure that won't be a problem. I should get a hefty price for it." Lacey sat stunned by all of this. Mark

CHAPTER 5

sounded excited, like this was something he really wanted to do. *Why would he do all this for me? I certainly do not deserve it.*

Their decision was to marry in two weeks. They realized it was quick, but they decided the sooner the better. Mark wanted to get the papers to Judge Cramson. He planned on timing them to arrive the day after they married; they would be delivered by courier.

Mark took a quick trip to visit his mom in Florida. Fortunately, Jessie had already filled her in on his upcoming nuptials. Of course, she was concerned for her son, but then she knew what a self-sacrificing person he had always been. She wanted to be certain that this was a decision he was making without any preconceived expectations. He assured her that he had no doubt that God wanted him to do this—he really did love her with all his heart.

Agnes, his mom, had a trickle of tears when he spoke of allowing Lacey to leave if she ever wanted to. "I'm not going to force her to love me, Mom. I hope that one day it happens but for now, I will wait." Agnes could simply nod. She knew her son was not only selfless but a gentleman. "Mom, I would like you to come to the wedding if you want to. It's going to be simple, probably in the Judge's chambers."

"Oh, Mark, I wouldn't miss it for the world," but the tears belied any enthusiasm. No, she wouldn't miss her son's wedding for anything. Oh, how she wished it was a normal wedding in a church. He had sacrificed so much for her and his sister for so many years. She just prayed that in time, Lacey would return his love. It sounded like her son was willing to wait as long as it would take for this to happen. She only hoped it would be sooner rather than later.

Lacey was taken aback when a limo pulled up to her house. She thought Mark would simply pick her up; this was a pleasant surprise. It gave her a flutter in her belly that he would be so thoughtful.

The wedding took place in the chambers of Judge Larsen. The only people that attended were Agnes, Jason, Jessie, and their children. Of course, baby Anna Beth was held in her momma's arms. Doug, Jason's brother and his wife, Molly, would have been there but they had two sick children and felt it would not be wise to travel with them. They said they would come for a visit when Lacey's baby was born. Jason's mom and dad, Ed and Patricia, were traveling in Europe and would come later with Doug and Molly.

Lacey was excited and wondered about the family she was marrying into. She had no family and had been on her own since she was nineteen. Her parents had been killed in an automobile accident, leaving her totally alone. Her inheritance from them was a house that she had to sell to pay off the mortgage. Her parents had just enough insurance to pay for their burials and enough left over for her to attend two years of community college. It was a difficult time in her life, but she managed to get through it. She still didn't know how, but she did.

Mark's breath was taken away when he took one look at Lacey ... his bride. She wore a pale green linen dress; the color captured the green of her eyes. Her hair was swept up in a beautiful loose chignon with fresh flowers woven around it. She was three months pregnant and did not have much of a baby bump. In fact, no one would even know just looking at her. She was beautiful. He wondered if she was even aware of how beautiful she looked. He often heard how a pregnant woman glowed; perhaps that was the reason. He could not help but believe she would look this beautiful even if she wasn't pregnant.

Agnes handed her a small bouquet of spring flowers to hold. She looked embarrassed to be standing here with Mark's family. This was the first time she met them. She couldn't believe the love and acceptance that flowed from them. This resembled a normal wedding with a very loving family.

She looked at Mark and her heart skipped a beat. He was the most handsome man she had ever seen, and he was about to marry her. No one could miss his broad shoulders and muscular frame. Even in his

CHAPTER 5

charcoal-colored suit, it could not hide his physique. He wore his fancy black alligator cowboy boots which looked expensive. His blue eyes looked piercing but warm and tender. From the first time Lacey had seen Mark, she was attracted to him, but nothing ever came of it. She had hoped that he would have noticed her, but he never did. Now, she was about to marry him ... who would have thought? She had no idea what he saw in her, but she would be forever grateful for what he was about to do. Without a doubt, she knew he was doing this for Dan, his best friend.

Jake stood next to his dad and was every bit the little gentleman. He wore a dark suit like his dad, and proudly wore cowboy boots like his uncle Mark. He was obviously excited to be at his uncle Mark's wedding. Jessie and Agnes wore beautiful linen dresses. The Judge entered and immediately looked at Mark, smiled, and nodded his head. It was obvious that Mark knew this judge; after all Mark was an attorney.

Mark did know Judge Larsen. In fact, he was a good friend and confidant of Marks'. He was a solid Christian and attended Mark's church. When Mark confided in him, and his plan to marry Lacey, Judge Larsen insisted on doing the ceremony. Mark had also shown him Cramson's letter and the document he wanted Lacey to sign, giving them complete guardianship of their grandchild with no rights granted to Lacey. The Judge was at a loss for words that two people could be so heartless.

Mark vowed to cherish and protect Lacey and her child until death parted them. He couldn't tell her he loved her, however. He knew he could show her, and this was one way.

Mark had written Lacey's vows; he did not want her to feel bound to him in the traditional commitment. She would be faithful and care for Mark as long as they were together. She thought it strange, but when she said them, she realized that Mark was giving her an out in the marriage. *Why would he think she would want out?* She knew she couldn't pledge her love to him, not when she had just lost her husband, someone she had loved for over three years. Maybe he would want out at some point. Well, she couldn't think of that right now. She had her baby to think of right now, and she would be forever grateful for what Mark was doing for her. A more selfless man she had never met.

Mark had to smile when Lacey gave her full name: Lacinda Marie McPherson Cramson. He could have a good time with that. The ceremony was brief, and when the Judge said you may kiss your bride, Mark leaned down and gave her a brief kiss on her cheek. When she looked up at him, her eyes glistened with unshed tears. He knew this had to be one of the hardest things Lacey had to do—marry someone she didn't love. If she only knew just how much he loved her, and the commitment he willingly made—he hoped that one day she would be able to return his love.

Jason took everyone out for dinner at an expensive steak and lobster restaurant after the ceremony. They all cheered when Mark walked in with his new bride. A pink flush crept up Lacey's face as she greeted everyone. This was a family that loved her unconditionally, and she had just met them. It was overwhelming to be with such a loving family. She could not explain the sudden longing in her heart; an emptiness she never realized was there was being filled—she was part of a family, a real family. Jake asked to sit next to the broom. They corrected him; "Uncle Mark was the 'groom.'". It didn't take long before Jake was up in Mark's lap. Lacy watched how Mark interacted with his nephew; she saw what a great dad he would be. She shouldn't have had any doubts.

Chapter 6

There would be no honeymoon or wedding night. Lacey had invited everyone over to her/their house after dinner. The family was staying at the Rosewood Mansion on Turtle Creek. Lacey knew it was a very upscale hotel in Dallas. Mark had moved all his belongings into her home two days prior. They agreed he would not be staying in her house until tonight. He had stayed at the hotel with his family until today. Mark had worked out the sleeping arrangements with her from the start so there would be no awkwardness. He did not expect anything from her. Right now, she could not think of anything so intimate. She still loved Dan, and Mark knew that.

Lacey loved entertaining, and Mark had been in their home many times. He knew where everything was in the kitchen and in the garage. He was good at barbequing, something Dan never liked. Mark always teased him that he was spoiled and used to having servants and eating at all those fancy restaurants. She laughed at the teasing and bantering that went on between the two friends. She realized that Mark missed her husband almost as much as she did. It would not be an easy adjustment, but perhaps not as difficult as she had thought.

She was taken aback when Jessie walked in with a small wedding cake. "Hey," said Jess, "we can't have a wedding without a cake." Everyone burst out laughing. "You put the coffee on Lacey, and I'll get this cake cut and served." The two women, now sisters-in-law, walked into the kitchen together. Lacey could not believe how comfortable she felt with

Jessie. They had just met, and she felt like she had known her for years. They were laughing about something when Mark walked in.

"What's going on in here? You know you have people waiting for cake, especially a little boy who is very anxious." Mark winked at Lacey, and she thought she would melt. *What is wrong with me?*

Mark walked out with the first two pieces of cake; one for Jake and one for his mom. Jake's eyes were like saucers when Mark handed him his cake. "Okay, buddy, why don't you sit up at the table and eat this. I'm sure Aunt Lacey would not appreciate having icing on her pretty couch."

"Aunt Lacey? Is she my aunt now? Like Aunt Molly?"

"Yep, just like your Aunt Molly. How do you like that?"

"I like it a lot, Uncle Mark. She's really pretty, like Aunt Molly and my mom."

"Yes, she is very pretty." Mark did not know that Lacey was standing behind him with the other pieces of cake to serve. She quickly ducked back into the kitchen. Hopefully, no one heard or saw what just happened. *Did Mark think she was pretty?*

Everyone came to the dining room table for cake and coffee. This time, instead of Jake asking for Mark to sit beside him, he asked if his Aunt Lacey could sit next to him. This really touched her heart. Lacey felt like her emotions were about to tumble out of her. This whole family was too much for her. They all knew of the arrangement and still they loved her. They all respected her and gave her the space she needed as she was still grieving the loss of her husband. *What mother would be okay with her son marrying someone he did not love— and know his bride did not love him?* Yes, they were an exceptional family and she never felt more loved.

After everyone had their cake and coffee, they were ready to head over to their hotel for the night. Not only Mark got hugs from his family but each one embraced Lacey as if they had known her for years. Even her new brother-in-law, Jason, hugged her as he welcomed her to the family. Jessie had given Lacey her cell phone number and Agnes did

CHAPTER 6

the same. Jessie had told her that anytime she wanted some girl talk to give her a call.

Mark started picking up the dishes and taking them to the kitchen.

"Mark, that's not necessary. I'll get these done in no time. I don't expect you to do dishes." Did he even hear her? He immediately started to rinse the plates off and loaded the dishwasher. "Mark, did you hear me?"

"Yes, Lacey, I heard you. You happen to be pregnant, and I don't expect you to be waiting on me or my family. I plan on helping as much as I can. You must take it easy and start eating. It was good to see you eat your whole meal tonight."

"You know, it's the first time I've been able to eat since I received the letter from Dan's father. I have to admit that I'm a little nervous at what his reaction will be when he gets your letter."

"Oh, I'm sure he will blow up. I ran the letter by Judge Larsen the other day, and he could not see anything in it that the Judge and his wife can fight us on; other than the fact that they can't have your child. I'm not even giving them visitation rights, if that's okay with you."

"I certainly do not want those evil people to even see my baby. How far do you think they will go? Can they insist on having visitation rights?"

"Yes, they can. And most courts would rule in their favor. They believe a parent cannot keep a grandparent away from their grandchild. That's why when you have given thought to my suggestion, you can, without any guilt, allow me to be the baby's father."

A big sigh escaped Lacey as she took the coffee pot to wash out. "You're right, Mark. I know I have more time to think about that decision—but watching you with your nephew and niece, I know you will be a great father to Dan's child."

"Thank you, Lacey. I promise I'll do my best. Well, I think you've had a big enough day. I know that I'm exhausted. Why don't you head up to bed? I'll lock up down here."

"Yeah, I am pretty drained. It was a big day. It's not every day I get married in a judge's chamber." She couldn't help the giggle that escaped.

She started to head for the stairs, turned slightly, "Mark, I'm sorry I can't be the wife you should have right now."

"Don't be, Lacey. I understand. I'm not expecting you to be."

Lacey could only give him a nod as she whispered, "Thank you. See you in the morning, Mark."

"See you in the morning, Lace. I hope you can sleep better than what you have been."

Lacey entered her bedroom and immediately had a heavy heart when she looked at the bed she and Dan had shared for the past three years. She stood motionless at her dresser. After what seemed like an eternity, she opened the glass jewelry box that sat there. She rolled her new gold wedding band around on her finger as she lovingly picked up the rings that Dan had given her on their wedding day. *Oh, Dan, I hope I have made the right decision. It certainly felt like it was the right thing to do, and I know Mark was your best friend. I know he's doing this for you and our baby. Should I put his name on the birth certificate? I wish I knew for sure. Good night, my love.* She closed the jewelry box, slipped on her nightgown and crawled into bed.

Lacey came down the stairs after smelling the coffee. Being pregnant, she tried to limit her coffee intake and allowed herself only one cup in the morning. For the most part, she drank decaf. When she entered the kitchen, Mark was seated at the table, dressed in khaki pants and a black polo shirt drinking a cup of coffee and reading something—was it a Bible? "Good morning, Mark." He looked up startled.

"Sorry, Lacey, I didn't even hear you come down. How did you sleep?"

"Better than I have for the past couple of months."

"I'm really glad to hear that. Hey, I ran to the bagel shop and picked up some bagels and cream cheese. There's also a bagel and egg sandwich. I wasn't sure what you like in the morning."

CHAPTER 6

"To be honest, I haven't been eating much breakfast since I've been pregnant. However, the morning sickness I had seems to have calmed down. Although, some smells still can set me off. I would love a bagel with some cream cheese, thanks a lot."

Mark stood up in a flash and went to the counter to get the box of bagels and cream cheese. "Can you have a cup of coffee, or should I make you a cup of herbal tea?"

"Mark, I can take care of myself, but a cup of coffee sounds great. Why are you all dressed up?" Lacey had come down in her robe and slippers and she still looked beautiful. Her hair was in a ponytail; without makeup he could see the freckles on her nose and under her eyes.

"It's Sunday and I thought I would go to church this morning. Unless you would rather I didn't. I don't mind staying home." *Home, that sounded strange even to his ears. He was in Dan's home not his.* Good thing he had spent so much time here that it did feel like home. At least he knew where everything was in the kitchen.

"No, that's fine. I think I'm going to just relax today. What would you like for lunch or dinner? I'm not sure what you're used to eating after church."

"My family invited us to join them at the hotel's restaurant before they head home. I told them I would ask you first before I made any commitment. Would it be too much time spent with my family if I pick you up after church?"

"Do you want me to join you? I really don't have to. I would totally understand if you would rather spend some alone time with them."

"I would love to have you join us and so would they." Mark couldn't help but notice the tears in her eyes. "I should be here about 12:30; they said they had 1:30 reservations. That should give us plenty of time to make it to the Rosewood Mansion. You will love it there; it's a beautiful five-star hotel."

"It sounds exclusive. Probably too rich for my blood."

"If not for my brother-in-law, I'm sure it would be too rich for my blood as well." Lacey had a hard time believing that. She knew with

Mark making partner four years ago, he was way up in the six figures. Her in-laws were wealthy, but she had never been invited, or included, in any of their uppity functions. Her husband never made it an issue. He never wanted anything to do with their lifestyle anyway. Dan said anyone with that much money was too stiff and critical for their own good. After spending time with Mark's family however, and all the wealth they had, they were not at all that way. Anytime someone had their own private jet, they had to be pretty well off.

Mark didn't wait for her reply, "Okay then. I'll pick you up at 12:30." He almost bent down to give her a light kiss on her forehead. It was tempting, but he thought better of it. He realized he would have a difficult time refraining in the days, weeks, maybe even months to come. It was going to be a long year and he hoped that's all it would be before Lacey could love him. *Who knows, it may be years, maybe never. Can I do this?*

Chapter 7

Mark sat in church wishing his new bride was sitting beside him. That had always been his longing, to one day sit in church beside his wife—and hopefully, one day have a couple of kids in tow. He knew it was best not to dwell on this or the longing in his heart. Mark attended a large church in Dallas, at least it was west of Dallas and not on the other side of town. He faithfully attended a men's study group on Wednesday night. It was quite large, but they broke up into smaller groups of six to eight men. The five men that he knew quite well had shared life together for the past five years. They knew of Mark's dilemma soon after he talked to Lacey. They had prayed for him and the decision he strongly felt God wanted him to make.

The associate pastor that led the entire men's group also knew of his heart's decision. Mark had met with Pastor James on several occasions to seek his wisdom and pray.

"Jim, I can't sit back and watch my best friend and the woman I have loved for five years lose their baby." He couldn't miss the raised eyebrow the pastor gave him when he had disclosed his love for Lacey for all those years. "Yes, I have loved her from the moment she walked into my office. After about a year, Dan asked if I would mind if he dated her. What could I say? I had an obligation to my mom and sister at the time and wanted to see them settled first. Dan was my best friend; I couldn't tell him no."

"Did Dan know that you had feelings for her?" asked Pastor James.

"Yes, and I knew I had to put those feelings aside. After all, I had never asked her out or acted on any feelings I had had for her. I gave Dan my blessing to pursue her if that's what he wanted."

"You're a better man than I am—I don't think I could not be jealous, even if he was my best friend." Mark simply smiled at the pastor and shrugged his shoulders.

"She was never mine to begin with. I was happy Dan found someone like Lacey. I know he really loved her. And how his parents have treated her is unconscionable."

Mark knew all too well what scripture taught about being unequally yoked, and he had made the decision that there would be no intimacy between he and Lacey until he knew where her heart was in her relationship to God. Was it too much to expect? Perhaps. He knew he loved her, and he was not afraid to share that with Pastor James and the men closest to him. They all knew he would love her unconditionally and wait patiently for her. Each of the men had patted Mark on his back, giving him their blessing.

Chapter 8

Mark was surprised how well the weekend had gone with his family. Brunch at the mansion was exquisite. It brought a smile to Mark's face when he thought of the excitement Lacey showed. The ice sculptures were phenomenal and the food exceptional. Lacey had never seen such opulence. Her eyes were like saucers as she took in the elaborate buffet tables. He had more fun watching her than he did enjoying the decadent meal. He could not fathom that the Cramsons with all their wealth had kept such an enjoyment from their daughter-in-law. He knew their lifestyle had to be over the top.

Mark had kept busy at work and almost forgot that he had a wife he should get home to. He gave her a call to let her know he would be leaving the office. He thought that was the considerate thing to do.

He never expected to walk into the house with an amazing aroma wafting through the laundry room. He was taken aback when he saw Lacey, his wife, standing at the stove preparing supper. "Man, that smells good. What did you make? I was expecting to order Chinese or some take-out."

"Mark, you are my husband, and I thought the least I could do is prepare supper for you. We're having baked pork chops and scalloped potatoes. Would you like corn, green beans, or broccoli?"

"Whatever you like. I'm not fussy, as I'm sure you'll find out." Lacey gave him a sheepish smile and went to the freezer to get a bag of frozen corn.

"Then corn it is. What can I do to help?"

"Nothing, dinner will be ready in about 30 minutes."

"Great! I'm going to take this monkey suit off and take a quick shower if that's okay with you."

"You go right ahead. I'll call when everything is ready."

I could sure get used to this— a beautiful wife—and she can cook. How lucky can a guy get? Mark took the stairs two at a time. He felt refreshed after his shower and put on a pair of shorts and a polo shirt. He bounded down the stairs just when Lacey was heading for the stairs to tell him dinner was ready. He almost collided with her as he rounded the corner. His arms spontaneously reached out to keep her from falling. "Sorry, I didn't see you, Lace."

Lacey took in a big whiff of him; he smelled fresh and oh so manly. His dark blond hair was still damp from his shower. She felt her face flush with him standing so close to her. "No, I'm sorry. I didn't expect you to be coming down the stairs just now. You were pretty darn quick with your shower. Anyway, dinner is served." She could not contain her giggle at that comment. "That sure sounded formal."

She had the table set and the pork chops and scalloped potatoes already on the table. The pork chops had been baked on top of the potatoes, and they looked delicious. Lacey went to the microwave and took out the corn. She had fresh baked rolls in a basket and asked Mark if he wanted a salad.

"No thanks. This is plenty, and it looks amazing. I actually worked through lunch and had a Snickers bar and a cup of coffee at about two o'clock."

"Well, that's not sufficient. Would you like me to make you a lunch in the morning?" A sad expression clouded her face when she asked that.

"Lacey, what's wrong?"

"Nothing. I always made a lunch for Dan almost every day."

CHAPTER 8

"Yes, I know. And I was always jealous of the lunches he had. I looked forward to the days you didn't, so we could go out to lunch. Much of the time we ate in the cafeteria together, and I would see what he had. He knew how to make my mouth water. I always teased him and tried to get him to share some of it with me. That never worked too well—he didn't like sharing."

Mark's comments seemed to lighten Lacey's mood. "I will make sure you have some of these leftovers for your lunch tomorrow, that is if you want them. You haven't even tasted my cooking yet."

"Sounds good to me, and I'm sure it's delicious. Before we begin, do you mind if I pray for our meal?"

"Oh, no. Not at all." Lacey bowed her head as Mark asked the blessing on the meal and for God to protect Lacey and her baby, and to keep them healthy. When she looked up at Mark, he couldn't help but notice the sheen in her eyes. "Thank you, Mark. I appreciate that."

The last thing he wanted was for Lacey to feel uncomfortable. He was thankful she didn't seem to mind him praying.

Their first evening together was rather quiet. Mark asked Lacey if she would mind if he watched a basketball game while she read. "No, I don't mind at all. Actually, when I read, I can tune a lot of sound out—you go ahead and watch whatever you like."

Mark stayed up to watch the news and Lacey went up to bed. He wondered if this is how their marriage would always be. *Patience, patience is what I pray for, God.*

He had started running once again in the early mornings. Lacey realized that must be how he kept in such good shape. Although, when he moved in, he had put his gym equipment on one side of the basement. As she sat at the kitchen table early one morning, she caught herself admiring his physique and honed muscles as he breathlessly came in the back door; his skin glistened with sweat. He was gorgeous to look at, and she felt guilty thinking that. His dark blond hair was tousled; his six-three frame filled up the room and he looked really good to her. She would not betray Dan, but it was certainly difficult not to stare at him. Mark said "Good morning" but quickly ran past her as a child caught with his hand in the cookie jar. She had no idea why he should be embarrassed.

Mark was thrilled to have a delicious meal each night when he came home. However, on Friday his calm and boring life took a turn. Mark had called Lacey each night, letting her know he was leaving the office. He did not think too much of it when she did not answer her cell phone; no doubt she was busy, so he simply left a brief message.

His stomach clenched when he got out of his car and smelled smoke. He burst into the laundry room and saw the smoke-filled kitchen. "Lacey!! Lacey!!" His heart began to pump so hard he heard it in his ears. He saw smoke billowing out of the oven. As quickly as possible, he grabbed a hot pad and opened the oven door ... more smoke poured out, causing Mark to cough and gag. *I believe we were going to have some kind of delicious casserole for dinner—instead it looks like a burnt offering.* He wanted to laugh but he was overcome with the need to find his wife.

"Lacey!! Lacey!!" Mark hurried out of the kitchen and into the dining room. *Where in the world could she be?* His heart continued to pump with fear that something had happened to her. He ran through the rooms downstairs and bolted up to the second floor, taking the stairs two at a time. He had never been in the master bedroom and immediately headed for her room at the end of the hall. As he burst through the doorway, he saw his wife lying in bed, her hand over her head. "Lacey, honey, Lacey." Mark was gripped with fear that she had lost the baby, or worse yet ... was dead. He bent down grabbing her shoulders and began to gently rub her arms. She woke and sat upright. When Mark looked into her eyes, there was not only confusion—it was obvious she had been crying. Her eyes were puffy and swollen.

"Oh, Mark. I'm so sorry. I must have fallen asleep. Why are you home?"

"I called your cell phone, but you never picked up. Did something happen to the baby?" Lacey shook her head. Mark scanned the room for some clue as to what caused her so much stress. His eyes settled on papers that had been strewn on the floor from her desk which was in

CHAPTER 8

complete disarray. "Lacey, tell me what's wrong." He walked over to pick up the papers and noticed they were bills. Immediately, Lacey was kneeling beside him taking the papers from him as quickly as she could. She began coughing and held her nose.

"Mark, do I smell smoke? Oh, no! Dinner!"

"Hey, don't worry about dinner. I think we're going out." He had the most adorable twinkle in his eye.

"Not good, huh?"

Mark couldn't hold back the laughter, "No, Lacey, it's not good. I'm not sure what it was supposed to be, but I don't think it's a burnt offering you had in mind."

"I'm so sorry. It was a chicken casserole. The recipe sounded good."

Mark glanced at the papers still in his hand. "Lacey, are these all your bills?"

Lacey grabbed what remained in his hands. "This is not your problem, Mark. It's mine."

"No, you're now my wife and your problem, is my problem. Now, tell me what needs to be paid."

Lacey looked up at Mark with watery eyes. "The bank is threatening to foreclose on my house." With this said, she burst into tears.

Mark wrapped her in his arms. "Lacey, tell me about it. I thought you were left the house."

"I was but I still had a mortgage to pay. Dan's parents gave him $200,000 for a down payment, leaving us with a $150,000 mortgage. I think his parents have some connections with the lending institution. I couldn't pay a mortgage payment until his $25,000 life insurance policy paid. I called and asked them to wait, evidently their answer is no. I've only missed two months but they're demanding payment or foreclosure." She sniffled trying desperately to hold back any more tears. Mark asked her if Dan had mortgage insurance. "He didn't think that was necessary with such a small mortgage. I don't know what I'm going to do."

"It's not what you're going to do, Lacey, it's what we're going to do." Mark took all the bills she was clutching in her hands. "Lacey, let's go downstairs. I think I need to open a window and get rid of some of the smoke. Breathing it in can't be too good for you in your condition."

Mark took her hand and led her out of the bedroom, down the stairs, and into the kitchen.

She gasped when she saw her casserole on the counter—burned to a crisp. "We could have had a house fire if you had not come home when you did."

Mark chuckled as he looked at the pathetic meal. "That's what I call crispy chicken. I think I'll throw the entire pan out if that's okay with you. I'll buy you a new one."

Lacey had to laugh as she looked at her blackened crispy chicken. "I guess we better go out."

It put a smile on his face to know he could make her laugh. It sounded so good. Mark had wanted to take Lacey out to a nice restaurant all week but didn't know how to invite her without it looking like an intimate time spent with his wife. "I know just the place to go. I think we can get in without a reservation." He knew that slipping the maître d' a bill would certainly get them in. "We'll go over these when we get home." Mark set all the bills on the kitchen counter.

Lacey took one look at what she was wearing and suggested she run upstairs and change. She didn't even wait for Mark's reply. She quickly put on a pretty yellow sundress and strappy sandals, put her hair up in a quick twist, and freshened her makeup. She returned to the kitchen only to find Mark going over all her bills. She was totally embarrassed. What would he think of her finances or lack thereof? He looked up at her when she entered. "Wow, I'm glad dinner was burned." He gave her a wink that spread warmth all the way to her toes. He didn't say one word about her bills but simply gave her a quick hug when he stood up. "It'll all work out, Lacey. Remember, I'm all in."

They had a wonderful meal. and it did Mark's heart good to see Lacey eat every bite of hers. Lacey shivered as they walked to the car. It had cooled off considerably since they had left the house. Mark took his jacket off without a word and placed it around Lacey's shoulders.

CHAPTER 8

"Thank you, Mark. I should have grabbed a sweater when we left. I know better than to leave the house without a wrap."

It was late when they arrived home, and Lacey looked exhausted. Mark must have read her mind; facing her bills was not something she was looking forward to. "Hey, tomorrow's Saturday. Why don't we wait and go over all the bills until then?"

Lacey not only agreed, she looked totally relieved. "Do you mind if I go to bed, Mark?"

It was ten o'clock, so of course Mark told her that he did not mind at all. "You go onto bed. I'm going to watch the news and check the sports channel." That was not his intent at all. He wanted to finish what he had started before they left for dinner. He could not understand how Dan had left her with such huge bills. He knew Dan didn't make nearly what he did but why did he spend what he did: huge mortgage payment, two vehicles, expensive gym membership, and he noticed a monthly bill for almost five grand. All of Lacey's bills would not be a problem for him to take care of; it was something he wanted to talk to her about anyway. Her situation simply elevated the conversation he had wanted to have with her all week.

Chapter 9

Mark was up early the next morning and went for a quick run. He got back right when Lacey was coming down the stairs. She looked adorable in a pair of shorts and a tank top. Her hair in a high ponytail, no makeup, and no shoes. He tried desperately not to notice how cute and fresh she looked. "If you don't mind, I think I'll head up to the shower."

"Of course, I don't mind." She enjoyed seeing him when he came in from his morning run. His hair messed, his muscles taut, and a sheen of sweat that made him look so masculine. *I know I should not enjoy seeing him like this. His wide shoulders and defined abs sure made it impossible not to notice such a handsome man ... all six feet three inches of him.* "I'll get the coffee going." Mark gave her a nod and ran up the stairs to shower.

Coffee was ready when he came down the stairs and Lacey was scrambling some eggs and had bacon frying in a pan. "Man, it smells good. You didn't have to make me such a big breakfast, but I'm not going to complain."

Lacey put the eggs in a pan and turned the bacon over. And that's when it hit her. Her stomach started to revolt. She was hoping the smell of bacon frying would not affect her—she was totally mistaken. She had her hand over her mouth and in seconds, she ran to the powder room off the kitchen. Mark started to panic. He had never seen anyone get sick like that. He immediately jumped up and turned the burners off on the stove. All they needed was a grease fire and for sure the whole house would go up. He quickly ran to the bathroom that Lacey was in. She had her head in, yes, actually in, the toilet bowl. "Oh, my goodness, Lacey. Let me help you." He immediately bent down and held her head while she emptied her stomach of last night's meal. Some of her hair had tumbled out of her ponytail. That's when he noticed how long it had to be. She always wore her hair in a ponytail or twist, never down. He pulled her beautiful hair back from her face and continued to hold her forehead.

"I'm better, thanks Mark. Man, I thought, or at least I was hoping, my morning sickness was behind me." Mark went out to the kitchen and brought her back a glass of water. She took a few sips and thanked him.

"So, that's what that was?" Relief evident in his response. "I was afraid you may have gotten food poisoning from dinner last night. What can I do? I turned off the burners on the stove so we wouldn't have a burnt offering for breakfast." Of course, he said this teasingly.

Lacey gave a weak laugh, and Mark did not miss the twinkle in her eye. "Can I make you some toast? My mom always gave me toast when my stomach was upset. I can fix you some tea and toast."

Lacey was touched by Mark's concern for her. Here she had just spent the last fifteen minutes puking, and he wanted to take care of her. She so wanted to prepare a descent breakfast for him this morning. That was the least she could do after burning their dinner last night and taken her to such a nice restaurant. He looked at her and saw she was crying. "I'm sorry, Mark. I wanted to have a nice breakfast for you—now you're taking care of me."

He gave her a gentle hug and wiped the tears away with his thumbs. "Sit down and I'll finish the bacon and eggs. If you want to get away from the smell, you can wait until I've eaten, and I'll air out the kitchen."

"No, I'm really fine now." She sheepishly looked at him and asked if he would mind fixing her a piece of toast and a cup of tea. "That actually sounds good right now."

Mark eagerly obliged and even gave her a large spoonful of scrambled eggs. "You need some protein, Lacey."

CHAPTER 9

"Thank you." She was touched by his kindness. Even knowing him for five years and spending a lot of time with Dan and him, she never would have expected him to worry about her so. She looked over at all her bills on the table and took a deep breath and sighed. "I guess I need to tackle these today."

Mark reached over and took hold of her hand. It wasn't awkward or uncomfortable since they had been such good friends for so long. "About the mortgage and your bills, Lacey, just hear me out before you say anything. I plan on paying off the mortgage." She started to protest but Mark quickly stopped her. "I'm also paying all these bills." He motioned to the stack of bills on the table.

"Mark, you can't do that. I will never be able to pay you back for what you're already doing for me. I cannot let you do this. I'll sell this house if I have to."

"Are you not by law my wife?" Lacey nodded in agreement. "Then, as your husband, you are my responsibility and the baby you're carrying. Lacey, I have the money, and I do not want the Cramsons to have any hold over you and your child. In fact, when I close on the condo, I'm putting that money in a personal account for you. That will be your money to do with what you want or need. Don't forget, this is my home now too. I'm not going to live here for nothing." When Mark looked up at her he saw the tears glistening in her eyes. "Please don't cry, Lacey. I've given this a lot of thought for quite a while—not just this week. I have a good reason now to take care of you." As he held her hand, he unconsciously rolled his thumb around on the top of her hand. Now she had more than sniffles … big fat crocodile tears began to slide down her face. He reached over and wiped the tears away with his other thumb. "Oh, Lacey, everything is going to be fine. You worrying over bills and a mortgage to pay is such a small thing."

She hiccupped as she tried controlling her emotions. "I'm so sorry—I think my hormones are all messed up. But why would you pay off the mortgage? It's not a small thing."

"Like I said, I don't want the Cramsons to hold anything over your head, and I have a feeling they knew you would not be able to continue living here. They want to squeeze everything out of you. I'm sure they would like nothing more than to wear you down, so you give up—I won't let that happen."

"Dan was paying his parents back for the $200,000 loan for the house. I should say, he was trying to pay them back. In fact, that was their agreement. He was determined not to owe them anything." Mark simply nodded. He now understood where all the money was going. "Well, one good thing. We haven't heard from them at all since they received your letter. That's good, right?"

"I don't want to worry you—I don't think we have heard the end of it. I'm sure they're not about to give up. Especially when they find out your mortgage has been paid." Lacey sat biting her lower lip; she was obviously thinking about what Mark had told her. "Lacey, we can't worry about something we don't know. We can only take a day at a time."

Mark stood to clear the breakfast dishes. That was a habit he seemed to have, always serving. He fixed Lacey another cup of tea and poured himself another cup of coffee. When he returned to the table, he took out his checkbook and started to pay her bills. "Mark, you know, I could sell this house. It's pretty big, and we don't need such a large home."

Mark looked up from his bill paying. "Is that something you want to do?" Lacey shook her head. "Then it's settled. This will be our home."

The house was quite large with four bedrooms, three and a half bathrooms, and a massive chef's kitchen with all the modern appliances one could imagine. The living room boasted a natural brick fireplace taking up much of the huge room and a formal dining room separated the living room and kitchen. The stepdown family room off the kitchen had a beautiful natural stone fireplace and there was a brick fireplace in the master bedroom as well. The basement was finished but still empty of any furnishings. Mark had told her that he would put his furniture down there once his condo sold. It was truly Lacey's dream house, and

CHAPTER 9

the thought of selling it saddened her. She was so grateful that Mark did not want her to sell. He could have easily suggested that, but he did not.

She was looking forward to decorating one of the four bedrooms as a nursery for her baby. At first, she and Dan said they wanted to be surprised as to the sex of their child; however, the more Lacey thought about decorating the nursery, the more she wanted to know if she would be having a boy or a girl. Just the thought saddened her; Dan would never know what his child would be. He said he wanted a girl just like Lacey, and of course, Lacey would tell him she wanted a boy just like his father … now that would never be. She secretly hoped her baby would be a boy and look just like his daddy, but then, Dan truly wanted a daughter. Just then the thought struck her—if it's a boy and he does look like Dan, it may be difficult for Mark to accept him as a son.

Each Sunday, Mark asked Lacey if she wanted to join him in going to church; each Sunday she declined. Mark never pushed her, but he continued to pray for her. He knew she was still grieving the loss of Dan—he also knew that God wanted to be her strength. After all, He is a God of all comfort and peace. But there was just so much Mark could do.

Mark did not know that every Sunday Lacey was checking out the wantads for a job. It wasn't until the middle of the third week of their marriage that she told him that she had a job.

"What? What do you mean you have a job?" Mark sounded a little miffed. "Lace, you know being married to me means you do not have to work." *This is the last thing I thought she would do as long as she's pregnant.*

"I know, Mark. But I need to do something. I can't have you totally supporting me when I'm capable of working and being home all day is a little boring. Besides, it's only temporary."

"Okay. Sorry, I got a little excited."

"Excited? You were a little angry I think."

"I guess. I don't expect a wife of mine to work ... especially a pregnant wife. Where will you be working?"

"It's for the law firm of Janson and Janson. Have you heard of them?"

"Yeah, I know Steve Janson; he's a good guy."

"As I said, it will be temporary. They need a receptionist for five months. It works out perfectly. I had an interview last Thursday, and they want me to start this coming Monday."

"Okay then. But I don't want you overdoing it... promise?"

"I promise. I'll still be able to make it home in time to have dinner ready for you." She was taken aback by his sincere concern for her.

"Dinner? I think we will be eating out or I'll pick up takeout. I don't expect you to run home and worry about having dinner prepared. You have already spoiled me."

"Me spoiling you? I think it's the other way around." Lacey felt like she could finally relax. She had no idea what Mark's reaction would be to her working, but she wasn't about to sit at home and do nothing. Mark was already doing so much for her.

Lacey was excited when Monday morning came, and she would start her new job. She had only a twenty-minute commute; it was perfect. She loved the office which they had shown her when she went in for the interview. It was only temporary since their receptionist had had quite extensive surgery and then would be gone for six to eight weeks of therapy. Lacey was even early for her first day and was greeted by one of the attorneys. It wasn't Steve Janson, who Mark had mentioned, but his brother, Larry Janson. "Good morning, Mr. Janson. Did you have a good weekend?"

"Good morning, Lacinda. Yes, I had a good weekend, thank you. I'm pleased to see you in early."

"Please call me Lacey."

"Okay, Lacey. I must tell you that we really won't be needing you after all. We hope this hasn't inconvenienced you too much. We will give you a check for the entire week. I'm sorry it hadn't worked out."

CHAPTER 9

Lacey sat there stunned. "It sounded like the perfect job, but I understand if you won't need me. I do thank you for the opportunity though." She stood up and shook the attorney's hand. Picking up her purse, she exited the building. *Well, that was strange.*

When Mark came home that night, he expected to see an exhausted wife anxious to go out to dinner. Instead, Lacey was in the kitchen preparing supper. "Hey, I thought you would be lying on the couch with your feet up. How was your first day on the job?"

"Mark, they let me go before I even started. Larry Janson said they wouldn't be needing me after all, and yet they're going to pay me for the whole week." Mark seemed awfully quiet, and she wondered if he had something to do with them not needing her. Maybe he had talked to Steve Janson. She knew Mark didn't want her working. It was all so strange.

As if he were reading her mind, "Hey, just so you know. I had nothing to do with this. In fact, I have not spoken to Steve in several months. But you're right, it is strange." *I wonder if Judge Cramson had anything to do with it.* "Several attorney offices work closely with the Judge and word must have gone out that you would be working for Janson and Janson. I wouldn't put it past him to keep them from hiring you." She looked sad and disappointed, but Mark had to admit, he was pleased she would not be working after all.

Four weeks after their marriage, Mark entered their home on a Friday night only to see his beautiful wife laying in a fetal position on the couch in the family room. She looked like she had been crying but was sound asleep. He gently rubbed Lacey's shoulder, "Lacey, Lacey, are you okay?"

Startled, she quickly opened her red puffy eyes. "Oh, Mark, I'm sorry I must have fallen asleep."

"Lacey, you've been crying. What's wrong? His eyes quickly roamed the table beside the couch. His eyes landed on a letter and a registered envelope. "May I read this?"

"Yes, of course." She nodded and reached for the letter. "It's from the Cramsons, and I don't know what I'm going to do. It's another threat. You were right when you said they were not going to give up."

Mark quickly read through the letter, shaking his head in disbelief. "Lacey, they absolutely cannot do this. I don't understand why they are so adamant. There is no way they can take your baby away from you."

Lacey looked up at Mark with such heavy lidded and sad eyes. She looked like she had run out of tears. Mark sat on the coffee table beside her and reached for her hand. "Lacey, the last thing you need right now is to worry yourself sick over all this. It won't help you or the baby. They obviously want to scare you into believing that they can take your baby from you. Believe me, they can't."

"Mark, I want you to be listed as the baby's father. Are you still willing to do that?"

"Yes, I am. The Cramsons will have to insist on a paternity test after the baby is born and hopefully by that time, they will have given up. Until then, we have to live our lives and make sure you and that precious bundle of yours stay healthy." Lacey looked up at him with a glimmer of hope in her eyes. "Lacey, do you trust me?"

"Yes, Mark, I do trust you."

"Good. Now let's go out to dinner. I can tell you're in no shape to do any cooking."

"But Mark, I have dinner started."

"Hush. What you started can be saved for tomorrow night, right?" She gave him a nod. "And besides, I like taking you out. Do you like Chinese? If you want, we can do take out." He did not want to put any pressure on her. Mark took one look at her expression and knew Chinese was not the answer to their food choice. "Okay, anything you have a taste for? I'm up for anything at all."

CHAPTER 9

Lacey looked sheepishly at him. "I do like Chinese but just the thought of it makes my stomach feel queasy. I would like a really good steak though."

"Sounds perfect to me, and I know just the place."

"Do I need to change clothes? Is this a fancy place?"

"You're fine just the way you are." Lacey was wearing white capris pants and a loose floral top. Mark wanted to tell her she looked adorable the way she was but thought it best to keep his thoughts to himself. He had noticed a slight baby bump but that, too, he kept to himself. If she wanted him to know—she would say something.

When Mark came down Sunday morning, he was surprised to see Lacey already dressed and sitting at the kitchen table. "Hey, good morning. Do you have plans for today?" Lacey shook her head. "Um, is there someplace I'm supposed to be?"

Lacey thought he looked so cute and embarrassed that he forgot plans that they may have had. "Good morning, and no, we have no plans. I thought I would go to church with you." Seeing his eyes light up warmed her heart. She never expected it to make a difference whether she went to church with him or not although, he never failed to ask her every Sunday. She got up from the table to pour Mark a cup of coffee and asked what he wanted for breakfast.

Mark went to the cabinet and took out the toaster. "I think I'll have an English muffin. How about you. Can I fix one for you?" Lacey shook her head in disbelief. "What? What did I say?"

"Nothing that you said, Mark. You are always taking care of me."

"Well, I'm up and I don't expect you to wait on me. Here, I'll put another muffin in the toaster. See how easy that was? Now you go sit." Lacey giggled at his gesture. He loved hearing her giggle and the fact that he was responsible for putting a smile on her face warmed his heart.

He wanted to do much more of that for her. Lacey was dressed in a very pretty sundress, one he had not seen before. "Lacey, you look very pretty today. Not that you don't always look pretty but I never tell you and I should."

"Why, thank you, Mark. I think I am starting to get a little baby bump, and it won't be long before I'll be the size of an elephant." She gave a big sigh, and then gave him a genuine smile. "I have a doctor's appointment in a couple of weeks, and I decided that I think I would like to know the sex of the baby. I keep calling the poor thing just baby, and it would be good to know." *Wow, this was the most she had ever talked about the baby to me.* He felt a lump form in his throat. *What do I say to all of this?* "I also want to paint the nursery, and it would be good to know how to decorate."

Mark was thankful for the change in subject. Painting he could understand, a pregnant woman, not so much. "I'm an excellent painter. Tell me the colors you want in the nursery, and I'll paint it for you."

"Oh, I think I can paint it myself. I have nothing to do all day."

"I don't think the paint fumes are good for a pregnant woman. You let me do the painting." Lacey's eyes began to well with tears. Mark reached across the table and took her hand in his. "You pick out the paint, and I'll do the painting. And no tears. Now eat your English muffin. I buttered it and you can put the jam that you want on it." Lacey took a deep breath and slowly let it out. Her emotions were really starting to get the better of her. "We should leave for church in about forty-five minutes."

"Boy, you can be bossy when you want to be." She gave him one of her cute giggles.

"Yes, I can be. Some things are non-negotiable."

Lacey could not believe how much she enjoyed being in church. It was all so new to her; the music was great, even if she had never heard any of

CHAPTER 9

the songs before. It certainly wasn't boring as she always thought church would be. She had never gone to church in her life, and sitting there for over an hour, she was sure it would be torture—but to her surprise it was good. The pastor's talk kept her attention the whole time. He spoke of God's grace and forgiveness. She sat there wondering what she had to be forgiven of. She was always a good person. She never stole anything, or killed anyone, or committed some horrible sin, so the whole idea of her needing forgiveness was something she had never thought of before.

The pastor read a verse from the Bible; she tried to remember what it said. He said it was from the book of Romans, wherever that was in the Bible. He said that everyone had sinned and fell short of God's glory. He said we all had missed the mark. There was nothing we could do in ourselves but that God in His love and mercy did it all for us by sending His one and only Son to die on the cross for us. He took our sins on him, every one of them ... past, present, and future. That was also something she had never heard of before. *I will have to ask Mark about that and what it all means.*

After church, several of Mark's friends came to greet her. They were all so nice and never looked at her in judgment. They must wonder what kind of a woman would marry a man just a couple of months after her husband died. She would certainly question someone's motives; however, no one seemed to care about that. Several asked if they would like to join them for lunch. Mark simply looked at her, allowing her to make the decision. She said it would be fine with her if that's what Mark wanted to do. They all agreed to meet at a restaurant not far from the church.

She had made some new friends, something she knew was grossly lacking in her life. She had one close friend, Tracey, who she really needed to call and tell her everything that had happened to her. She had attended the funeral for Dan, and Lacey had to admit she was embarrassed to tell her that she was married again. *How do I tell people without going into the horrible details of my situation?* Tracey had called many times after the funeral but Lacey had never returned her calls. Her friend finally gave up calling, and she couldn't blame her. Having new friends was exciting, but she still needed to reconnect with Tracey.

When they returned home after lunch, Lacey wanted to ask Mark about the pastor's talk but then changed her mind. She knew she would sound dumb asking him her questions. Mark was so confident and knew so much; she wondered how she could start the conversation. She opted to take a nap instead. However, later that evening, as they sat together in the family room, Mark asked her what she thought of the church service. Lacey's eyes lit up. *This was what she was waiting for. How did Mark know all she needed was to be asked; now she could comfortably ask him and hopefully, Mark would be able to give her an answer.* "Oh, Mark, I enjoyed the music and I especially liked meeting all your friends."

"I hear a but coming," said Mark.

"I do have a question about what the pastor said." Mark nodded and told her to ask away. "Well, he said that we have all sinned, and we need God's forgiveness. I don't understand that. I haven't committed any sin that I'm aware of. I think I have always lived a good life, even if I never went to church. I lived by the golden rule. You know, do unto others as you would have them do unto you. I've always been good with that—so how is it that the Bible says that I have sinned?"

Mark asked her to wait just a minute while he ran to where he had left his Bible on the kitchen counter. When he returned, he sat down beside her and opened his Bible to Romans 3. He asked her to read the chapter. Then he asked her to read Romans 3:23 again. She did so, "'for all have sinned and fall short of God's glory.' Mark, that's the same verse the pastor said." She looked up at Mark with sadness in her eyes. "If I'm a sinner, then what hope is there for me? And what about you, Mark? There's no way you have done anything wrong. Why you're the example of a perfect man; you're good, you're kind, you're selfless."

Mark was quick to hold up his hand and stop her right there. "Lacey, I may in your estimation be all those things, but God calls me a sinner. All of us have sinned. There is only one perfect man and that's Jesus Christ. When Adam and Eve sinned in the Garden of Eden, sin entered

CHAPTER 9

the human race. Every single one of us has inherited a sinful nature. Do parents have to teach their child to say no, or mine?" Lacey shook her head. "That's right, they never have to teach that. It comes naturally. Jeremiah 17:9 says that the heart is deceitful above all things, and beyond cure. Who can understand it?"

"But everything I had said about you is true, Mark. You are the most unselfish person I know. Just look at what you are willing to do for me and Dan's baby?"

"Hey, that doesn't mean I haven't sinned or don't sin on a daily basis."

Lacey gave him a wry look. "You? What kind of sin are we talking about? We're not talking about murder or stealing or some other horrific sin. Right?"

"Lacey, we don't have to do anything like that to be a sinner. We are born with sin, but I can look at my life on a daily basis and find sin." He wondered just how much he should reveal to her about his life. "I can harbor unforgiveness in my heart when I've been wronged or bad thoughts towards the guy that cut me off in traffic when I drove home today." *My desire to claim you as my wife and make passionate love to you.*

"Pfft, that's not sin."

"Isn't it? It's not what God would be pleased with. But I also know that God forgives even the slightest sin. I first have to acknowledge that I am a sinner and in need of God's forgiveness. It says in the Bible that if I confess my sin, He is faithful and will forgive my sin and cleanse me from all unrighteousness. But God didn't leave us in our sin. John 3:16 tells us that He sent His one and only Son, Jesus, to die for us."

She was certainly listening to everything he said. However, he was at a loss as to her understanding all that he had read and told her. He knew it would take God to speak to her heart before she came to realize her need of God's grace and forgiveness. He decided that he would back off and allow her to think about what he had said. They would talk some more but he wanted her to understand her need for a Savior. After all, if you think you have no sin, then why need a Savior? *I'm sure she will see her need in time; until then I have to be patient and continue to pray for her.* The last thing Mark wanted was to push her away. He was thrilled that she even wanted to talk about it and had joined him at church.

"I think I'm going to head up to bed if you don't mind."

"Of course, I don't mind. I'm going to see if there's a game on." Lacey went up to her room and Mark remained in the family room to watch some TV. His heart was heavy for Lacey and before even watching any television, he spent some time praying for her.

For the next few weeks, Lacey accompanied Mark to church. She found that she really looked forward to Sundays and spending the time with Mark's friends. They always liked to talk about the sermon at lunch and she listened to every word they said. She had questions but was too shy to ask the group although she knew she could talk to Mark anytime. She loved his friends and realized for the first time that she actually had friends. His friends loved her and accepted her as one of their own. It blew her away.

Chapter 10

"Mark, I know I told you that I have a doctor's appointment next week. I've decided I really want to know the sex of my baby. Are you still willing to paint the nursery for me?"

"Yes, of course. When you find out, we can go and pick out the paint." This put a smile on Lacey's face and seeing her smile, put a smile on Mark's face. He wanted nothing more than to see her happy. There were times when he looked at her and she was just so sad looking. She was unaware of how often he saw her wipe tears from her eyes. Naturally, she was still grieving the loss of her husband. He missed his best friend as well. He knew Dan would want to see his wife happy again—he was just that kind of a guy. Mark had no idea how many doctor appointments she had been to since they were married. This was the first she mentioned one. After all, what did he know about pregnant women? Eventually, he would have to talk to his sister or his mom. Just watching her lose her breakfast a couple of times was enough to make him wonder why any woman would even want to get pregnant.

They were married over two months now and Mark hoped they were home free from the Cramsons' interfering in Lacey's life. He was wrong. A letter showed up registered mail on Monday. He came home from work to a trembling and shaken wife.

"I thought it was too good to be true when I hadn't heard from these wicked people." She handed Mark the letter. Once again, it was filled with threats that they would be at the hospital at the birth of their grandchild. The baby would be handed over to them. They had proof that she would be an unfit mother. As he read the letter, Mark could only shake his head in disbelief. "Mark, I'm so scared. Can they really do that?"

Mark sat down beside her on the couch. *Would she object to him holding her?* His heart said no. But then, what did he have to lose anyway? They had been friends for a long time, so she was no stranger to ever getting hugged by him. He gently pulled her into his arms—she came willingly. He held her close while she sobbed into his shirt. Being almost five months pregnant, Lacey was finally beginning to look pregnant—to Mark she was fragile. He rubbed her back and whispered that everything would be okay.

She pulled back from him. "How can you say it's going to be okay? It's not. I know it's not going to be okay! Why do you keep telling me this?!" Now she was angry, and he couldn't blame her.

"I'm trusting in a powerful God to work this out. He already knows what the outcome will be, and I have to trust him with you and the baby. He loves you and He loves your baby even more than you do." She laid her head back on his chest as she allowed the tears to flow.

When the tears finally subsided, she looked up into Mark's beautiful blue eyes. Lacey had to shake her head for even noticing his gorgeous eyes. "Mark, I'm so sorry. I didn't mean to lash out at you. I'm just so terrified that they're really capable of doing such a horrible thing. I can't lose my baby."

"I know. And you're not going to lose our baby; I mean your baby."

"Oh, Mark, that's okay. If this baby is not taken from me, it will be our baby." She sniffed and hiccupped after all the crying she had done.

Wow, I never saw that one coming. Mark continued to hold Lacey. He knew it was something he longed to do for the rest of time. *Will it ever be?*

CHAPTER 10

Monday came with Lacey looking forward to her OB appointment. She had only mentioned to Mark that her appointment was today but she did not give him any details as to the time or where her doctor was located. Her appointment was at ten o'clock in Dallas. She allowed herself plenty of time, leaving at nine. She turned her radio on when she left the house. Of course, she had to get on the highway heading to Dallas. Once on the highway, she kept up with traffic, always a cautious driver. A car pulled alongside of her but kept getting closer and closer to her. She moved to the outside lane, but the car followed right alongside of her. *What was this jerk trying to do?* She didn't panic until her car was bumped. Lacey gripped the steering wheel with all she had. The car hit her again, jarring her whole body. Cars were honking and she was panicking. She could slam on the brakes, but a car was right behind her. The car hit her one more time, and she was forced off the side of the road, headed for the steep ditch. She felt the car tumble several times, unconsciously she clutched her stomach—then all went black.

Mark was sitting in a chair beside the hospital bed. He could not help but stare at how beautiful she looked. He never got to see her hair loose; it was always in a ponytail or twisted up somehow. Now it splayed across her pillow flowing down past her shoulders. The auburn color was breathtaking. He never had noticed all the golden highlights that streaked through it. He wished he could see her amazing green eyes. There was no doubt in his mind just how much he loved her.

As Lacey regained consciousness, she wondered where she was. At first, she had no idea where she was. She looked to her side and was relieved to see Mark sitting there. Panic took hold of her emotions—her voice quivered. "Mark, what happened? My baby? Is the baby okay?"

As soon as Lacey said something, Mark was at her side. He lovingly held her hand in his. "Lacey, you were in an automobile accident. You've been unconscious until now. Do you remember anything at all?" She had a puzzled look on her face as she shook her head.

Mark had panicked when he received the phone call that his wife had been in an automobile accident and would be taken to Baylor

Hospital. He had rushed over as quickly as possible. In a way, he was hoping a cop would have pulled him over so he could have gotten a police escort to the hospital but that hadn't happened. By the time he checked in, Lacey had already been admitted to the ICU.

As her memory slowly returned, he could see confusion in her eyes. "I … I was on my way to my doctor appointment." She glanced out the window; it was completely dark outside. "What time is it anyway?"

"It's five in the morning." Mark saw the tears begin to well up in her eyes. One blink and huge crocodile tears rolled down her cheeks. "Do you remember what happened? Anything at all, Lacey?" He gently brushed the tear away with his thumb.

"I kind of remember a car bumping into me. At first it kept getting closer and closer and then I pulled into the outside lane, but it came alongside of me again … hitting me over and over again. I kind of remember looking in the rearview mirror but I couldn't stop because a car was directly behind me. Before I knew it, I was on the shoulder. I think I lost control. I started to roll over and over—that's all I remember. What happened to my car?" She tried moving in the bed but couldn't. "Mark, why can't I move?"

"The doctor does not want you to move too much. And being unconscious, he was afraid you might do so, especially when you started to regain consciousness. They don't want you to lose the baby." Lacey gasped when she heard that. "Right now, the baby is doing fine. They have you snuggled in a contraption to keep you still. You're going to be pretty sore for a while, but you have no broken bones, a few bruises, and probably one pretty bad headache." As he held her hand, he managed a wink, along with a comforting smile. "I'm going to tell the nurses that you're awake. And as for the car? I'm buying you the safest SUV out there." She couldn't help but melt at the wink he gave her.

Lacey felt her heart constrict. *Could I be falling in love with him? Is that possible? Oh, Dan, what do I do? There is no way he can possibly love me. As far as Mark's concerned, I'm only his best friend's wife who he promised to take care of until the baby is born.*

CHAPTER 10

Once in the hall, Mark walked towards the nurses' station; he had heard quite the commotion—anger spewing from raised voices. The closer he came, he recognized the Cramsons' voices. *What in the world were they doing here? And at this time of the morning?* Then he heard, "Do you know who I am? I'm a superior court judge for the state of Texas! I demand to know if my grandchild survived the crash!"

"I understand, sir; however, with the HIPAA law, I am not legally allowed to provide that information."

Mark stood back and listened to the exchange. It wasn't long before a doctor, along with security, came to give support to the poor nurse in question. "Is there something I can help you with, sir?" asked the doctor upon his arrival.

"My daughter-in-law and my grandchild are in this hospital, and my wife and I demand to know the condition they are in." The doctor took the clipboard from the nurse, his eyebrows raised as he read the information. "Sir, you are not listed as someone entitled to this information. I will have to ask you to leave the hospital."

"What do you mean I'm not entitled to this information? I am her father-in-law."

The doctor motioned to security. "If you do not leave, security will have to escort you out."

Mrs. Cramson began to cry and carry on as if she couldn't bear not knowing the condition of her "precious daughter-in-law." This demonstration was to no avail as security gently took hold of their elbows and began to move them away from the nurses' station.

As soon as they exited the doors, Mark walked up to the doctor. "Thank you for sticking to the law, Doctor. They are two people we do not need to have here. They were Mrs. Hamilton's in-laws, but no longer. In fact, we are involved in a tough situation with them. They have threatened to take Mrs. Hamilton's baby from her the moment it is born." He heard the nurse gasp upon hearing such an announcement. "May I take a look at that clipboard?"

The nurse handed it to Mark, and he was thankful to see that Lacey had had the foresight to give specific instructions that the Cramsons would not be allowed to have any information regarding her health or the health of her baby. He was listed as the only person allowed to have this information. He never knew that she had done that. Right after their marriage, Mark had put Lacey on his insurance plan and had given her an insurance card. His chest puffed up a little with the fact that she trusted him with all her health information.

"Oh, by the way, I came to tell you that Mrs. Hamilton is awake. Of course, she is concerned about the baby." Mark was in the room when they did the first ultrasound while she was unconscious. When Mark had arrived at the hospital, he had told them immediately that his wife was pregnant. They did not waste any time doing the ultrasound. In fact, he had to admit that he was unsure if he should stay in the room while they did the test. He had hoped that he wasn't crossing any boundaries in their relationship. It was a privilege to see this amazing little life growing in Lacey's womb. It took his breath away. He was not about to tell Lacey the sex of her baby. She would find out when they did the next ultrasound. "Doctor, how soon before Lacey can have another ultrasound? I know she is anxious to know how the baby is and also the gender. She was going to find that out at her OB visit yesterday."

"I'm heading in there now and will let her know that I'll schedule one for some time this morning." Mark gave a nod and accompanied the doctor to the room. Lacey's eyes were closed when they entered but immediately opened them when they walked up to her bed.

"Hey, how do you feel?" Mark reached for her hand. She didn't say anything; her sad eyes said it all as they landed on the doctor.

"How's my baby, Doctor?"

"I think your baby is going to be just fine. The last ultrasound showed a strong, healthy baby. I'm going to schedule another one this morning and if it all looks good, we'll get you out of this contraption so you can move around."

CHAPTER 10

"Oh, I don't mind staying in this as long as my baby is safe." The doctor patted her arm and said he would be back later in the morning. He looked like he could use some sleep, and Mark was sure that's where he was headed. Lacey took one look at Mark and thought he looked as tired as the doctor. "Mark, you look like you could use some sleep." In spite of his current appearance, she thought he was the most handsome man she knew. He looked cute with his messy hair and disheveled clothes from sleeping in a chair. She loved the rugged stubble look on his handsome face; he was always so clean shaven. "Why don't you go on home?" However, she didn't sound very convincing. Mark was not about to leave her alone in this hospital room, especially with the threat that the Cramsons could easily try again to get past the nurses' station.

"I got some sleep in the chair last night. I probably look a sight though. I'll head on home after your ultrasound." He wanted to be there when she saw the sex of her baby ... Dan's baby. A sudden pain gripped his chest, and he couldn't understand why. Was it because it was his best friend's baby or was it because it wasn't his child? Either way, he had a fierce protectiveness of Lacey and her unborn child. He would do anything to keep them safe. He couldn't believe that the Cramsons had been there insisting on knowing how Lacey and the baby were. The more he thought about it, he wondered how they even knew she had been in an accident, that was a puzzle too. He was beginning to see several red flags in this whole situation.

Mid-morning and they had not been in for the second ultrasound. Mark told her that they were probably busy— he assured her it would take place so they waited patiently. Lacey had fallen asleep again and Mark sat reading a magazine. The TV was on, but he kept the sound low. To his surprise, in walked his sister, Jessie, and her husband, Jason. "Wow, I never expected to see you guys here." He was up immediately giving them each a warm embrace. Mark was pleased to have their support. It had been a long couple of days.

His sister spoke up, "You can't very well call with the news that Lacey had been in an accident and expect us not show up here for you."

Mark motioned for them to walk out of the room to a visitor's lounge. Jessie took a good look at her brother, "Mark, you look like you have not slept in a week." He gave her a wearisome grin. "Tell us what happened."

Mark agreed that he probably looked pretty bad. "You're right, I haven't slept in almost two days." He ran his fingers through his thick hair hoping he could make it look a little better. Obviously, it didn't work. He proceeded to tell them what he knew of the accident and what Lacey recalled. What's even worse, the car that hit her took off. The witnesses never got a good description, let alone a license plate number.

Jason and Jessie could only sit and shake their heads. "That's unbelievable," said Jessie. "How could no one not catch the make of the car or at least the color."

"Too many people only think of themselves and their inconvenience that they won't take the time to stop."

Mark had to agree with Jason and then began to tell them of the Cramsons' visit. Jessie and Jason were shocked that they even showed up. "Yeah, they insisted on seeing Lacey or at least finding out how she was and "their" grandchild. It's weird because I have no idea how they would even have known about the accident." He told them about the last letter Lacey had received and all the threats she had had.

"Man, do you think they had something to do with the accident? Why would they be so adamant about getting the baby from Lacey?" Jason could not stop with the questions.

"That's just giving me the creeps, Mark." Jessie shuddered at the thought of this being something so nefarious. "Does Lacey know they were in the hospital?"

"No. And I'm not going to tell her either. It will really freak her out. Let's get back before she wakes up. I know she's anxious for the ultrasound and hopefully the tech will be in soon." Jason and Jessie followed Mark back to Lacey's room, but they did not enter immediately; something was amiss as soon as Mark walked into the room.

CHAPTER 10

Mark's breath stopped as soon as he entered and saw Judge Cramson standing over Lacey's bed. Mark immediately stormed towards him. "What are you doing in here?"

"Oh, Mark, my boy. It's good to see you." He reached out to shake his hand, but Mark would have none of it. "Um, I just came by to see how my daughter-in-law is."

"Your ex-daughter-in-law. You are not on her list. You nor your wife. You are not allowed to even be in here. You better leave."

"You're forgetting that I am a superior court judge for the state of Texas." His eyes were raging, and he looked like a man totally unhinged.

"You'll leave now, or I'll call the authorities." Mark looked down at his wife and saw that her eyes had opened—panic evident in her face. Mark reached for her hand and held it firm in his grasp. "Leave... now!" The Judge turned and left without another word. Mark saw Lacey's waterfilled eyes and his heart broke for her. *God, hasn't she been through enough?*

"Mark, what was Judge Cramson doing here?" She looked confused and helpless.

Not wanting to scare her more than she was already, Mark tried to make light of the Judge's presence. "Oh, I guess he's just concerned about you. Maybe he feels responsible for you in some way ... you were Dan's wife."

Jason and Jessie walked in as soon as the Judge left—they had heard everything. Jessie immediately gave Lacey a hug and told her how sorry they were she had been in an accident. "Mark, what's that man's problem?" asked Jason.

"I wish I knew. All I know is that I want to get Lacey home." Just then the doctor and the ultrasound tech came in. "Hey, Lacey, look what's here? You've been waiting for this." He couldn't help but notice the juxtaposition of emotions in Lacey's eyes. "Hey, I'm sure it's all going to be fine."

"You've told me that before." She then gave him a knowing smile.

The tech got the ultrasound in place and began to prep Lacey. Mark, Jason and Jessie, went out in the hall and waited. Mark did not know if Lacey would even want him in with her, so he resigned himself to staying with Jason and Jess. As he waited, he strained to hear a little of the conversation. He heard the tech: "Okay, my dear. Let's take a look at how baby is doing." For some reason, Mark's heart was pounding out of his chest. He already saw the earlier ultrasound, but for some reason he felt like this was the first time.

"Wait. Before you start, I would like my husband to be in here with me." Jessie gave Mark a knowing smile and a-thumbs-up. Mark's eyes glistened as he winked at his sister; he heard the tech ask him to come in.

When Mark entered the room, Lacey reached her hand out for Mark to take hold of. His heart thumped in his chest. The tech began and looked at Mark, "Mr. Hamilton, I know you—" Mark discreetly shook his head. He did not want Lacey to know that he already knew. She quickly cleared her throat, "would like to know the sex of your baby." Mark started to correct her but felt Lacey squeeze his hand.

"Yes, of course. We can't wait to know. I know Lacey has been anxious to find out." He stood by her side watching the monitor. The tech pointed out the baby's heartbeat, the tiny legs, arms, and then she moved to the torso.

"And here SHE is. Your baby girl." Lacey gasped as the tears began to slip down her cheek. Mark reached over and wiped her tears with his thumb but continued to hold her hand with his other hand, not letting go.

"Lacey, you're having a girl!" He said with such enthusiasm; the tech gave him a quizzical expression.

"Mark, we're having a girl." Lacey was quick to acknowledge the fact that Mark's name would be on her and Dan's baby's birth certificate. Mark gave her a wink, and she could not help but notice the sheen in his eyes. She realized he was touched by her acknowledgement. Her heart swelled; more than ever she wanted him to be her baby's father.

CHAPTER 10

The doctor came in and did his own exam with the ultrasound. "Lacey, your baby is perfectly healthy and fine. I think we can remove this pelvic stabilizer and allow you to get up and move around. I would like to keep you one more night, and hopefully, we can release you tomorrow. How does that sound to you?"

"It sounds wonderful. I'm so happy my baby is okay." The tears started once again but this time she looked at Mark and mouthed the words "thank you." She felt so protected by this strong handsome man. She knew she could trust him completely. He may be doing this for his best friend but right now she felt cherished and protected.

The equipment, tech, nurse, and doctor left the room, leaving Mark alone with Lacey. Jessie and Jason came in after they left. It was obvious that Jessie was as excited as Mark and Lacey. "I'm going to be an aunty to a beautiful baby girl! Lacey, I'm so happy for you." She bent over the bed to give her a hug.

"Jessie, Jason, when did you get here?"

"We arrived a little bit ago. And I'm so happy we were here when you had the ultrasound."

Lacey took a look at her husband and giggled. "Mark, you look like you have not slept at all. Since I'm going to be here another night, why don't you go home and get some rest."

"I agree with Lacey, Mark. You look pretty scroungy—so unlike you. No wonder Lacey giggled at you. Why don't you and Jason go on home. At least you can get cleaned up."

Mark leaned over the bed and gave Lacey a kiss on the top of her head. "Okay, then. I'll clean up and look my handsome self when we return." He loved hearing the giggle escape from Lacey's lips. "Now, now, don't you know it's not nice to make fun of someone who has spent the past couple of days sleeping in a hospital chair?" Lacey shook her head at him.

Leaving with his brother-in-law gave Mark the opportunity to talk openly without the concern that Lacey would overhear their conversation. He expressed his concern and how Cramsons knew Lacey had been in the auto accident. "Jason, what are you thinking?"

"Mark, it's certainly a puzzle. The bigger question is why they are so adamant about taking the baby away. Can you think of anything Dan may have said about his in-laws?"

"No, not at all. Dan was in my office the day before he went on his climb. In fact, it was an amazing time. I had asked Dan that if he didn't make it off the mountain, would he know where he would spend eternity. He said he had no idea but that he wanted what I had and the assurance that he would go to heaven. Jason, it was incredible to pray with him and I know beyond a shadow of a doubt that I will see my friend again."

"Wow! That's incredible. And that totally was God speaking to you to even ask him that."

"Yeah, I know. I had talked to him many times before, and he never even gave a hint that he was interested. It really was God speaking to his heart and preparing him to accept this final invitation, and I'm so glad he did."

"You said his parents had a twomillion-dollar insurance policy on him?"

"Yep. That's what Lacey said. His parents were supposed to change the policy to Lacey being the beneficiary, but they never did."

"That sounds fishy if you ask me. Do you think they cashed the policy and collected the two million?"

"Lacey seems to think so."

"What do you think of me calling Detective Malone? Remember, he was the detective that helped Doug and me find Molly—the same one that Doug contacted to help us find you. He's a good guy."

"Hey, I never gave that a thought. Maybe he can dig something up on the Cramsons. I can't believe that they have no motive for what they are doing to Lacey. Granted, she said they never did like her because she wasn't good enough for their son. What they are doing is certainly beyond understanding."

CHAPTER 10

"What's not to like about Lacey? She's a sweet, beautiful woman. Jessie and Agnes fell in love with her immediately. I can see why you fell in love with her all those years ago." Mark felt his chest tighten. Yes, he did love her for over five years but never once acted on it. She may not ever love him back, not in a true marital sense, and that would be a hard pill to swallow.

Once home, Mark ran upstairs to shower and shave. The bed sure looked inviting; however, he was anxious to get back to Lacey. When he came downstairs, Jason was on the phone with Detective Malone. He hoped he would take his case. Malone was in New York and this was Texas. Although, having his own detective agency, he could probably take on a job anywhere. Jason ended the call and told Mark that Malone would take the job. He would fly out sometime next week. Mark breathed a sigh of relief and was thankful Jason had suggested Malone. "I wonder if I should tell Lacey or wait until Malone is here. I don't want her overly worried." Jason agreed with Mark but thought he should at least let her know before Malone came out. "I agree. I just don't want her stressed out. I don't think that would be too good for her or the baby. I can't believe she's having a girl."

"You're both having a baby girl." Mark shook his head and gave a strained laugh. "Hey, you're gonna be a dad, Mark."

"Yeah, I guess so. Who would have thought?" It suddenly hit him in his solar plexus that he was going to be a father. His stomach tightened to the point he felt nauseous.

"Hey, are you okay?" Jason didn't miss how quickly Mark's coloring changed to a chalky gray. "You better sit down. I'll get you some water." Mark heard Jason's chuckle as he left for the kitchen. This was not funny.

After giving Mark the glass of water, Jason suggested he lay on the couch and get a few winks. "No, I would rather get back to Lacey. And don't you dare tell her what just happened. She would think I'm a real wimp; the news of being a father has me scared to death."

"Your secret is safe with me. You look a lot better than you did; at least you don't look like you slept in your clothes for a week. Come on, I'll drive us back to the hospital; you can relax." Mark tossed his keys to Jason.

Mark was thrilled when they entered Lacey's room. She was up and walking around. She could not help but notice the smile on Mark's face when he took one look at her. "Wow, it's great to see you up and walking. Can we go home now?"

"I only wish. The doctor wants me in one more night and hopefully, tomorrow morning, I can go home. For now, he wants me to get used to walking. I can't walk by myself in the hall but if you walk with me, I should be fine."

"Not a problem. I would be happy to take you for a walk. Where's your leash?"

"Very funny, smart guy." She said this with a twinkle in her eye. Both Jessie and Jason said they would wait in the room while the two of them went for a walk.

Mark immediately took Lacey's arm and laced it through his. He felt the zing all the way down to his toes. He wondered if Lacey felt it too. It felt so right, and the connection warmed his heart.

Lacey did not realize how much she was beginning to depend on Mark. She could not allow thoughts of Mark being more than her protector to even enter her mind. *Once all this craziness with the Cramsons is over, he'll want an annulment. I just have to accept that. He has his life to live and one day he will find someone to truly love. I know he's doing this for Dan and his baby; I may never understand why.* She looked up into Mark's eyes and shuttered at how incredibly handsome he was: he was a good six or seven inches taller than her and she was five-eight. With his incredibly broad shoulders, he filled out whatever shirt he wore beautifully. You couldn't miss the dimple in his left cheek when he smiled; and oh, that smile, he could definitely melt ice cream. His beautiful blue eyes were so warm and caring. She felt so safe with him by her side. *What was that unexplainable reaction her body just had when Mark put her arm in his? Can't be anything.* Lacey had to shake the thoughts that were running rapid through her head. *He's Dan's best friend; they had a*

CHAPTER 10

special bond and that's the only reason he's willing to sacrifice so much of his life for me. After all, it may only be a year out of his life—perhaps that's how he viewed it. She had to focus on herself, and her baby ... her baby girl. *No, our baby girl. That's what she told Mark and for now, she would be our baby.* In no time, they were standing outside her room. She was exhausted, but with so many thoughts running through her head, it made the walk easier. He gently got her situated back in bed.

He melted when she looked at him with those beautiful emerald green eyes of hers; he saw gratefulness but something more ... or was it his imagination?

Chapter 11

Lacey was tired but so happy to be back home. So was Mark after one more night of sleeping in a hospital chair. Mark's sister, Jessie, offered to stay a couple of extra days although, Jason had to get back to New York. He said he would send the company plane to pick her up. Lacey was grateful to have a woman who had already experienced giving birth twice; however, she expressed concern about Jessie not being home with her own children. She assured her that Jake and Anna Beth would be fine; Jason's mom, Patricia, was more than willing to stay with the kids. Patricia was amazing with the children, and Jake adored his grandma from the very first time he met her.

Once Lacey was settled, Jessie came downstairs to sit with her brother. She saw the concern in his eyes. "Mark, what seems to be the problem?" He was always amazed how well they could read each other's minds. However, it was usually the other way around, and Mark would always sense when Jessie ruminated over some concern or dilemma she was faced with.

"I don't know, Jessie. I can't stop thinking about the Cramsons and what they are doing to Lacey; the bigger question is why. I know they never approved of her and Dan getting married." Jessie grasped her chest. "It's true. They never thought she was good enough for him. The heart-wrenching part of it—Lacey had always known."

"Mark let's think about this. This grandchild would be their only heir. Maybe they simply want to make sure the child would always know them and be a part of their lives."

"Could be. But I think there is more to it than that. I don't understand the cruelty they have shown Lacey. Jess, they have been merciless and downright evil. And I am convinced they were a big part in the near-death accident Lacey experienced."

"Do you really believe they would want Lacey dead … and their grandchild?"

"Not their grandchild, but I honestly believe they want to see Lacey either dead or give up her baby to them. Why now that's the mystery. Especially knowing how horrible they were to Dan." Mark rubbed his hand through his hair, and Jess could not help but notice the frustration and weariness in her brother's eyes.

Suddenly, Jessie's eyes lit up. "Mark, who went climbing with Dan? I hate to even think it, but what if Dan's death was not an accident?"

Mark shook his head in disbelief. "Jess, I don't know who he went with other than the usual guys. Dan talked of them, but I can't say I know any of them. I don't think I can even remember any of their names. I'm sure Lacey knows who they are. I'll have her give me their names and phone numbers."

"I'd wait until tomorrow before I would ask her about it. She's pretty exhausted right now. Didn't the doctor tell her he didn't want her going up or down stairs for the next two weeks?"

"Yeah, he said for sure the remainder of this week and possibly the next. He told her that when I was in the room with her. She didn't look too pleased about it. I know she'll do anything to protect her baby."

"I'll be sure and take care of her today and tomorrow but after that I'm going to have to get home. You'll be on your own caring for her. Do you think you can manage, or should you hire a home nurse to come in and look after her?"

"What? No way. I'm sure I can manage. I already notified work that I would not be in for a couple of weeks. I told them I would work from

CHAPTER 11

home with no problem. Any court dates, I'm going to push back a few weeks. That shouldn't be a problem."

"I'm going to go check on her, Mark, to see if I can get her anything. I'll get supper ready for us. What's in the freezer that I can prepare for tonight? Hey, I know. I'll make my lasagna, and that way you can have leftovers tomorrow."

"That works for me. You know I can only do bagels." Jessie told him she knew he could do more than that. "Once your lasagna is gone, I'll do carryout. You know, they have a lot of restaurants doing deliveries these days. I can easily do that. Someone's always thinking and that's a great idea for someone like me." Brother and sister shared in their laughter.

Jessie went upstairs to check on Lacey. She was fast asleep, so she quietly exited the room and went back downstairs to start supper. When she peeked in the family room, she saw her brother stretched out on the couch, out like a light. She understood how stressful the past few days had to be for both of them.

Mark had called one of his buddies in his small group from church and was shocked when calls started to come in; everyone asked when they could bring a meal over for them. When he told Lacey, she was overwhelmed with their concern and love for her.

"I can't believe they want to do this for me. Your friends are incredible, Mark. I barely know them."

"That's just what people do when someone has a need within the body of believers."

Jessie had flown back to New York, and Mark had cared for Lacey on his own. Granted, he was exhausted from running up and down the stairs after one day. He delivered breakfast to Lacey and brought his coffee up on her tray. He thought he would sit and keep her company while she ate.

"Mark, thank you so much for the way you have taken care of me. You look tired, and I'm so sorry. This is not something you bargained for."

"Lace, I told you I was all in, and I meant it. I've been able to do quite a bit of work from home."

"No wonder you look exhausted, you're working and taking care of me."

"You look pretty exhausted yourself. It's not fun for you being holed up in your bedroom these past few days." Just then a light bulb went off in Mark's head.

"Mark, what in the world are you doing?"

He took her tray and set in on the nightstand. "I'll be back for this." He slipped his strong arms under Lacey's legs and with the other he reached around her back.

"Mark, I'm almost six months pregnant and way too heavy for you. What are you doing?"

"I'm taking you downstairs. You need a change of scenery, and I need to have you close to me. Now hang on." Lacey wrapped her arms around his neck. She felt the intimacy of such closeness immediately. He carried her as if she weighed nothing.

When he got her downstairs, he carried her to the family room and sat her on the couch. He put a couple of throw pillows behind her and stretched her legs out. "Now, I'll even give you the remote. You can lay here and watch TV." He ran upstairs and brought her breakfast down. He brushed the hair out of her face that he had messed up in transport. "There, how's that?"

Mark hadn't noticed, but Lacey was about to burst into tears. This man was incredible. She bit her bottom lip to keep the tears at bay. He brought her a muffin, scrambled eggs, and a cup of herbal tea. "Lace, would you like me to butter your muffin? It's a blueberry muffin, the one you like from the bakery."

"I think I can butter my own muffin. Mark, you are doing way too much for me." She immediately turned a beautiful shade of pink. He gave her a wink that melted her toes. Too choked up to say much more,

CHAPTER 11

Lacey shooed him away and told him he could go get some work done while she ate.

"I know when I've been dismissed." Unconsciously, he bent down and gave her a light kiss on her forehead. "I'll check on you in a little bit."

Lacey sighed as he turned to leave. It may have been a simple kiss, but the touch of his lips lingered on her forehead. *How did I get so lucky?*

Chapter 12

Mark was holed up in his office all day, other than making a couple of quick sandwiches, one for him and one for Lacey. He had waited for the right time to ask Lacey about the men that Dan had gone climbing with. "Lacey, I was wondering if you knew the guys that Dan went climbing with?"

"Yes, of course I know them. Not well. Why?"

How do I even broach the subject? God, give me wisdom here. "My sister asked if I knew any of the men. She brought up something that I never thought of and, um ... she wondered if any of them even checked his equipment before and after the accident." Lacey gave a puzzled look and then her hand immediately covered her mouth.

"Oh. No, Mark. Are you saying what I think you're saying? I've known Jeremy for a long time. I believe Steve was the other guy he climbed with. I don't think Dan knew him for too long; he had climbed with them maybe one other time. I can't imagine anything so despicable on either of their part."

"Hey, I'm not accusing anyone. Maybe his equipment was defective. He may not have thought to check it out thoroughly. I would like to call one of the guys. Do you have a phone number for either of them?"

Lacey got up and went to her address book in the desk. She immediately got Jeremy's information and gave it to Mark. He couldn't help but notice her clouded eyes. The last thing he wanted was for Lacey to be upset or even think of the possibility of foul play. *She has had enough stress in her life to last a lifetime.* "I'll give Jeremy a call later tonight." Mark was really hoping Lacey would want to go to bed early so he could make the phone call when she was asleep.

Mark stayed in his office the remainder of the day. When it was time for dinner, he came into the kitchen only to find Lacey putting something in the oven. "Hey, what are you doing?"

"Mark, I think I can manage making dinner for us. In fact, someone brought us a delicious casserole that I found in the fridge. The name on the sticky note said it was from Susan. Is this the Susan we have gone out to lunch with after church?"

"Yep. One and the same. She's married to Jack. When they heard about you being in the hospital and sent home on bed rest, which by the way, you are not doing right now, they insisted on bringing us a couple of meals. The other couples also brought meals for this week and next." Lacey could not believe the kindness of so many people that she barely knew. She had never heard of such a thing. "Here, move out of the way and take a seat at the table, or do you want to eat at the couch. I'm fine either way."

"I think I would like to sit at the table if that's okay with you." Lacey opened the cabinet and started to reach for the dinner plates when Mark quickly, but gently, took her by the shoulders and led her to a chair. She huffed her response, rolled her eyes, and gave him an exasperated look as she sat down, knowing it would get her nowhere.

After dinner, Mark insisted that Lacey lay on the couch. She didn't seem too anxious to go back to her bedroom. If he didn't get his call to Jeremy tonight, he would call in the morning. He wanted to contact him before Detective Malone came out. Fortunately, Malone's arrival was not until the following week. He did not think Lacey was in any way prepared to meet with him.

Once the kitchen was cleaned up and the leftovers put away, Mark went to the family room to sit with Lacey. No surprise to him, she had fallen asleep watching a chick-flick. Mark removed the remote from her hand and changed the channel. He was sure she would wake up as soon as he put a ball game on but she didn't stir. Mark ran upstairs and turned her bedding down so he could lay her in bed.

After he returned downstairs, he noticed that Lacey never even stirred. "Hey, sweetheart, let me get you in bed." Bed, his imagination took him to the hope that he really was taking her to bed—his bed. He had to shake his head from that thought. *Man, I really love her.* He lovingly put one arm under her legs and the other under her shoulders. He chuckled when her arms automatically reached up around his neck. He knew she was still asleep.

Mark tucked Lacey into bed and returned to the family room. He did not waste any time calling Jeremy. "Jeremy, this is Mark Hamilton. I have to admit this is an awkward phone call. I worked with Dan Cramson. He was my best friend. His wife, Lacey, gave me your number."

"That was such a tragedy. I still can't believe Dan is gone. The three of us climbed together for the past two months; Dan and I had climbed together for a couple of years. What can I do for you?"

"Like I said, this is an awkward phone call. A few of us have a question about Dan's equipment after the accident. Do you know if the authorities investigated the cause of death thoroughly?"

There was silence, and Mark wondered what was going through Jeremy's mind. "I know all of his equipment was taken as evidence. Each of us were questioned quite extensively. It was the first time Dan's brother, or I guess step-brother, ever joined us for a climb."

Mark felt his heart begin to race. "What? Are you saying Dan's step-brother, Jude, climbed with you guys?"

"Yeah. It was the first time any of us ever met him. We didn't even know he had any siblings; he never talked about him."

"So, when you climbed, were you all together?"

"When it's been just the three of us, we stick together. His brother suggested he and Dan climb together—Steve and I climbed, and each spotted for the other. They were probably about 20 or 30 feet parallel to us. Man, everything was going well until we climbed to 300 feet, so close to the top. It was something that I'll never forget. His scream was deafening. Steve and I looked in horror when we saw Dan laying at the bottom."

"What did Jude do?"

"He definitely looked shocked and scared to death. I had my phone out and dialed 911 immediately. When we climbed down, Jude grabbed Dan's rope and carabineers."

"How long did you wait for emergency to get to you?"

"Maybe 20 or 30 minutes. The three of us just sat there in shock. As soon as we got down, I went over and felt for a pulse. I knew with one look that he was gone. His neck was snapped and, oh, man, it was just horrible. I'll never forget the way he looked. Steve and I stood in disbelief for a long time; we couldn't keep the tears from falling. I would consider Dan to be an expert climber. His equipment would have been flawless. Dan was a good guy, one of the best."

"What about Jude?"

"Jude?"

"Yeah. Did he show any emotion? Did he seem shook in any way?"

"I honestly couldn't tell you. Steve and I grieved together. We sat on a rock close to the body ... Dan. It was tough." There was a long pause, and Mark realized this had to be difficult for him. "The hardest for me was telling his wife. Steve and I drove to the house. Of course, when I told her the news, she collapsed, and I carried her to the couch. My wife came over as soon as I called her; that's when Steve left. My wife, Sara, sat with Lacey until way into the night. She offered to spend the night with her, but she insisted that she would be all right. I told Lacey that I would pick up her car in the morning."

"The police took all your statements at the scene?"

"Yes, they spoke to each of us separately."

"So, Jude had to give his statement as well."

"Yeah. I saw him speaking to an officer."

"Did they take Dan's equipment?"

"As far as I know, his step-brother gave everything he had to them. What's going on? Are you a cop, an attorney, or something?"

CHAPTER 12

"I am an attorney, but it has nothing to do with Dan's death. I would really like to meet with you sometime where I can better explain our concern. I don't know where you live but I'm in Arlington."

"You're close. Do you know where the Aroma Coffee Bar is?"

"I know the place. It's not far from me. What's a good time for you?"

"If we can meet early tomorrow, I can make it before work, say six? Unless that's too early for you."

Mark knew there was no way Lacey would be awake by then. "I'll see you at six then. I'll be wearing khaki pants and a black Polo shirt."

He heard Jeremy chuckle. "Good point. I would have had no idea who I was looking for."

Mark was pleased with the conversation he had with Jeremy. Knowing Dan's stepbrother was there really gave him pause. *Why in the world would Jude even be there? Malone would have his work cut out for him when he got here.*

Jeremy had no problem spotting Mark. He waved as soon as Mark walked into Aroma Coffee Bar. The two shook hands and immediately, Mark felt comfortable with Dan's buddy. "Hey, thanks for meeting me here. I know it's last minute." They each ordered their coffee and found a table near the back of the coffee bar.

"After our conversation last night, there was no way I would miss meeting with you. I called Steve immediately, and he wished he could have made it this morning. He was flying out on business this morning."

"I felt there was something I needed to tell you—over the phone did not seem appropriate. I have no idea how well you know Lacey or the situation she is in."

"I haven't seen her since the funeral. My wife called her a couple of times. She never seemed to want to talk much. A few times she left a message, and Lacey never returned her call. I think she finally gave up calling."

"Lacey and I married three months ago." The shock on Jeremy's face was priceless. "Let me explain why she even agreed to marry me." Mark began telling him, without going into too much detail, what precipitated his marriage. He told him of the threat to take her and Dan's baby and his suggestion to marry her. "Did you know that Dan's father is a supreme court judge for Texas?"

"Wow. No, I had no idea who his dad was. He never really talked much about his parents. I didn't even know he had a stepbrother. That's incredible. And you're okay married to Dan's wife? I guess you could call it a marriage of convenience. That's quite the sacrifice you're making."

"I don't look at it as a sacrifice. Dan had been my best friend since college and then law school. I have known Lacey since she started working at our firm." He noticed Jeremy's raised eyebrows. "It's strictly a platonic relationship. I know she still loves Dan. I could not see Lacey lose their baby. I'm willing to stay with her as long as she wants me." He paused for a moment before he added, "I really felt it was something God was telling me to do." Jeremy nodded in understanding. He paused, wondering if he should tell him more—Mark decided he had disclosed all that was necessary. "I would appreciate it if you wouldn't mind leaving this information between the two of us. I would rather not Steve know all these details."

"Not a problem. I told Steve only what you mentioned to me last night, that you were concerned if the police got Dan's equipment to examine. No need to tell him all the details."

"Thanks. I know you have to get to work and I need to get going as well." Mark was not about to tell Jeremy that he needed to get back to Lacey before she woke up. That was no one's business but his. They walked out together and shook hands before heading to their cars.

Chapter 13

Mark cared for Lacey without complaint the remainder of the week. He carried her downstairs in the morning and back up the stairs in the evening. When Lacey woke that first morning, after falling asleep on the couch the night before, she was determined to be awake when Mark carried her to her room. Oh, she certainly did not mind being carried; however, she was embarrassed to put Mark in that position. She did not believe that he would want that kind of intimacy; no, it was better to be awake when he carried her to her room.

On Sunday morning, Lacey knew Mark would be going to church. He had asked her on Saturday if she would mind if he went. She told him she had no problem with him going and to make sure he thanked all their friends for the food they had provided all week. She had first told him to thank his friends which he quickly corrected and told her they were *their* friends. This truly warmed her heart. She hated to admit to him that she never had many friends.

Lacey told Mark that she would stay upstairs until he came home. After he brought her breakfast and told her goodbye, she headed for the shower.

She put on a pair of sweats and loose top, put on some makeup, and put her hair up in a messy twist. She had wanted to start cleaning out some of Dan's drawers; she knew this would be a sad time. She was avoiding this task and although she had cleaned out his closet, except for a couple of his favorite shirts, today was a good day to tackle the drawers. She was pleased Mark had gone to church so she would have this alone time.

First was his armoire. She had not touched anything in these drawers. She took everything out: underwear, socks, t-shirts, pajamas, and neatly stacked everything in piles on the floor. She caught herself sniffing his t-shirts hoping she could get a whiff of the cologne he always wore. Everything smelled of laundry freshener and had a good clean smell. She was disappointed that nothing she smelled reminded her of Dan. However, the few shirts in his closet did, and she would not part with those.

Lacey went to his nightstand. His good watch was still in there. She knew he would not wear his Rolex when he went climbing. She was surprised to see a Bible when she opened the drawer. *I never knew he even had a Bible.* She opened the first page and was shocked to see Mark had written something on the first page. "*On April 6, 2019, my best friend and now brother in Christ, gave his heart to the Lord. I know God has great plans for your life. Friend forever, Mark.*" The tears began to flow, and Lacey did not know why. *What did this mean? He gave his heart to the Lord?* She had never heard of such a thing. It touched her heart that Mark had given Dan a Bible. *God had great plans for his life? Really. How could that be when he died the very next day?*

Her mind went back to the evening before Dan left to climb. He seemed so happy and told her that when he came home from their climb, he had something exciting to tell her. *Could this have been it? That Mark gave him a Bible?* She sat on the floor and started going through the pages. She found Romans, the book that Mark read from a couple of weeks ago. She had no idea how long she sat there and read. The Bible said that she was dead in her trespasses and sins. How could this be? She was a good person … wasn't she? She read and cried and read some more. She heard Mark coming up the stairs. What time was it anyway? Had she read the Bible all this time?

CHAPTER 13

"Lacey, Lacey, are you up here?" He stood at her bedroom door stunned to see her on the floor. "Lacey, are you okay?"

She wiped her eyes; it was obvious she had been crying. "Yes, I'm fine. I found this Bible in Dan's nightstand."

Mark came in and sat beside her on the floor. "That's the Bible I gave him. It was the day before he went climbing. I had the greatest privilege of my life praying with Dan to receive Christ." She noticed a few tears escape and roll down his cheeks.

"Oh, Mark, losing Dan had to be just as hard for you. I'm so sorry. I read what you wrote in here. Please explain what it means."

Mark could not help but think of the Ethiopian eunuch as he rode in his chariot reading the book of Isaiah and asked Philip to explain what he was reading. Mark took both of Lacey's hands and held them in his. Her hands were trembling; he wanted her to feel secure and comfortable with him as he explained the decision Dan had made. It was the most important decision of his life.

"Lacey, remember when you asked me about our Pastor's message a few weeks ago?"

She nodded. "Yes, I asked you what he meant by saying that we have all sinned. I have thought a lot about what you said and what I have been reading in this Bible."

"That Friday morning, Dan came into my office so excited. He told me that you were pregnant; he was on cloud nine. He then told me he would be climbing the next day; he even invited me to go with them." He chuckled at the remembrance and shook his head. "I told him I wanted my feet firmly planted on good old terra firma." This brought a chuckle from Lacey. "I asked Dan, what if he never made it off that mountain, if he knew where he would spend eternity." Mark took a deep breath before continuing. He quickly prayed that God would give him the wisdom and the right words. She sat and stared at him the entire time.

"Mark, what was Dan's answer?"

"Dan told me he had no idea where he would spend eternity. He only said he wanted what I had. I asked him if he wanted to surrender his life to Jesus and he said, yes. He said he wanted, no needed, to do that. We immediately went to our knees, and Dan prayed right there. He acknowledged that he was a sinner and needed a savior." Lacey nodded as if she understood everything he was saying. "Lacey, that was the most important decision Dan could have made. I know without a doubt that I will see him again."

"But Dan was a good man, Mark."

"Yes, he was. But being good does not save us. How good is good enough? If I could gain heaven by being good, how do I know when I have reached ultimate goodness? And if I could simply be good, then Jesus would have died in vain. Lacey, God sent His son so I would not have to work at being good enough. He took my sin. He paid the price I could never pay. The Bible says in Isaiah that our righteousness, or all my goodness are like filthy rags. It is only by what Jesus did on the cross and the grace he has poured out on us that we can know God. He pursues us. I can't earn it by being good."

"Mark, what do you mean that you will see Dan again?"

Mark took the Bible he had given Dan and went to the book of John. Lacey had noticed that a lot of words in this Bible had been highlighted. Now she understood; it had been Mark's own Bible. He began to read John 14:2: "My Father's house has many rooms; if that were not so, would I have told you that I am going there to prepare a place for you? Lacey, why don't you read the next verse."

"And if I go and prepare a place for you, I will come back and take you to be with me that you also may be where I am."

Mark took back his Bible and flipped a couple of pages. "Lacey, here is another passage from John 11:25 and 26." He began to read, "'Jesus said to her, I am the resurrection and the life. The one who believes in me will live, even though they die; and whoever lives by believing in me —believe this, Lacey?"

CHAPTER 13

He could see that Lacey was trying to process everything they had just read. She nodded and with eyes swollen with tears, she told Mark she too wanted what Dan had received. Mark was sure his heart was about to explode out of his chest. He took Lacey's hands in his and asked her if she wanted to pray to receive Christ as Dan did. She nodded, and immediately, without him saying a word, Lacey began to pray. It was a simple and heartfelt prayer; she acknowledged her sin and her need for Jesus to come into her heart. Mark followed by praying for her and thanked God for the opportunity he had of sharing God's grace and forgiveness with her. Her tears were real and so were his. He could not help it—he immediately pulled Lacey to his chest in a warm embrace. Silently, he thanked God for giving him the greatest desire of his heart: Lacey trusting Jesus to come into her heart. His joy was without words as he continued to hold her; without thought, his hands had begun to gently caress her back—he trailed them up and down in a slow reverence.

When he realized how intimate things had become, he quickly pulled back. He had to remind himself that he was here to protect Lacey and Dan's unborn child. She may never love him, and not the way she had loved her husband.

Lacey was embarrassed and knew Mark was only there because of Dan. Yet, he held her as if she were the most precious gift he had been given. She had to admit, it felt good to be in his arms and cherished. She hoped that one day perhaps things could be different; could he ever love her? He was a wonderful man and deserved a wife that would love him completely. She had to let those thoughts go. Right now, she was just so happy that she had made the decision to allow Jesus into her heart. She felt relieved that she could put to rest the Romans 3:23 verse that had been troubling her for weeks: "For all have sinned and come short of God's glory." All have sinned, and that included her.

Chapter 14

Mark cautiously lifted Lacey to her feet. At six and a half months pregnant, it was obvious that she was self-conscious of her large round belly. "I'm sorry, Mark, I should never had sat on the floor to begin with." She unconsciously stretched her back which caused her tummy to protrude even more. Mark was quick to get behind her and immediately began to rub her back. "Oh my, that really feels good. Thank you."

"Now I'll carry you downstairs but before I do, I want you to find something nice to put on because I'm taking you out for a steak dinner. We are going to celebrate what you just did. I can't tell you how special this is, but I think you know."

Lacey not only nodded her head but gave him a hug and tender kiss on his cheek. "Yes, Mark, this is very special. I can't begin to tell you the joy I feel right now. But I think we still have a couple of dinners in the fridge that we could have."

"That's not gonna happen. We can always have them tomorrow. Now, you go change and I'll wait in my room."

When Lacey stopped by his room, she looked sheepish and uneasy as she looked at him. Mark was surprised at how in tune to her emotions he seemed to be lately. *Must be from spending all this time with her.* "Lacey, what seems to be the problem?"

"Mark, look at me. I don't seem to fit in any of my clothes. This sundress is the loosest thing I have that looks decent. I think I've gotten bigger since I have been home. I have only worn sweats or a robe for two weeks."

"Lacey, you look beautiful to me. I think it's time we go shopping for some maternity clothes. Hey, instead of you trapesing through the stores, why don't you shop online. It's easy and they'll deliver it right to the door. Many times, it's delivered the next day."

"That sounds wonderful. I never gave that a thought. I have always been one to run to the mall for anything." Well, with her budget, she had not been to a mall in quite some time. She did wonder how she would be able to pay for anything.

Their dinner that night was wonderful. Lacey was touched by Mark's thoughtfulness. When they returned home, Mark knew he needed to talk to her about Detective Malone. He would be coming to Texas next week to meet with Lacey and him. Mark asked Lacey if she would mind taking a seat on the couch. He noticed her trepidation as she sat down. The last thing he wanted was for her to feel uneasy. They had just had the best time together, but he felt it was important he give her a heads up.

"Lacey, remember when I asked you for the phone numbers of the friends Dan went climbing with?" Lacey nodded her response. "My sister suggested I ask Detective Malone to investigate Dan's death." He heard her gasp, and he immediately took both her hands. "Lacey, it may not amount to anything. I simply want some answers. I don't think it's a coincidence that you were forced off the road—and then Judge Cramson showed up at the hospital."

"Okay. I understand where you're going with this. Maybe Dan's death wasn't an accident. But I can't believe that his own parents, or anyone for that matter, would do anything so terrible."

"I can't either. That's why I felt it important that we called in a private investigator. Malone will be here sometime next week. I wanted you to be prepared. No doubt, he'll have a lot of questions and would definitely want to question Dan's friends. I'm sure you're not aware of this, but Dan's stepbrother, Jude, joined them that Saturday."

CHAPTER 14

"What? Dan never said anything about him going on the climb. I wonder why he asked him to join them?"

"I have no idea. All I know is that they seldom talked to each other. Perhaps Dan was trying to reach out to him the best way he knew how." Lacey sat very still, and Mark wondered if she was even listening to him. "Are you tired? It's been a big day. I don't know about you, but I enjoyed tonight."

"Yes, it's been a big day, but a very good day. I never knew I could have so much peace. Even talking about Dan's death, I feel like I have peace knowing that he's in heaven. That is truly the hope that we can have. Before, when I would think about him being gone, I shivered thinking he was lying in a cold, dark grave. Knowing that there is hope beyond the grave is certainly something I can think about without feeling cold and empty myself. If you don't mind, would you help me up to bed?" Lacey felt awkward asking him to carry her and right now it was the best way she could think of to be held in his arms. "I think I would like to go to church next Sunday. I believe there are only a couple of steps leading into the church. I'm sure I can handle those without you having to help me. I want so much to be there. After all, I have so much to celebrate."

"Then you will be there." Mark gave her a wink that melted her heart a little bit more. "Yes, I think you're right. Maybe only three steps at the most."

"I have a doctor's appointment coming up. I should be getting another ultrasound, and I'm sure my, I mean our, baby is just fine." She couldn't help but notice the contented smile on Mark's beautiful face. *Where did that thought come from, his beautiful face?*

Without another word. Mark picked up Lacey and carried her up the stairs to her bedroom. When he set her down, he held onto her just a little longer. They looked into each other's eyes. Lacey was certain that Mark was going to lean down and kiss her. Was she even ready for this? As quickly as the moment came, it disappeared, and Mark left her alone in her room. Lacey knew it had to be this way. She had to admit, if not to anyone else but to herself, she was lonely. *Oh, Dan, I miss you so much. I'm so sorry that I barely think of you anymore. I no longer see your face at night when I close my eyes; instead, I see Mark's handsome face ... always smiling, always caring. What would I do without him?* Lacey had to shake all these thoughts from her head. She could not dwell on something that could never be.

Mark walked out of Lacey's room, his heart pounding so hard he was sure Lacey could hear it. *What in the world was I thinking? I almost kissed her. I must be the world's biggest idiot. I cannot allow my heart to get involved. Once I no longer have to carry her up and down the stairs, I'll be able to control my desire for her.* Who was he kidding? Every day was getting to be more and more difficult.

Lacey was excited to be in church. It was her first Sunday after praying to receive Jesus. She felt like her heart was soaring to the skies; it was glorious. She was greeted by their friends and many who had brought them a meal. Going out to lunch with them was so refreshing, after being homebound for two weeks. However, when they returned home, she had to admit she was exhausted. She fell asleep on the couch in the family room. Mark had gone upstairs to change into a pair of shorts, and when he returned, he was not in the least bit surprised to see her fast asleep in the couch. This brought a smile to his face. He loved looking at her beautiful face. And being asleep, meant she had no idea how much he loved staring at her. He went to his office to catch up on some work.

By the time he returned to the family room, Lacey was still fast asleep. Mark shook her lightly. He was afraid she would not be able to sleep that night. "Lacey, Lacey, sweetheart, it's five o'clock." Her eyes fluttered open, quicker than he thought they would. *What would she think if she heard me call her sweetheart?* He called her that before, but knew she was not aware of it.

When she opened her eyes, she simply gave him a sweet smile. She never said anything about the endearment, but she heard it. It warmed her heart to hear such a loving word come from his beautiful lips. Lacey immediately shook her head; she could not allow this to take root in her heart. Mark was only being his usual self ... very kind and thoughtful.

CHAPTER 14

"Lacey, I'm afraid you won't be able to sleep tonight."

"How long have I napped?"

"Napped? You slept for three hours; it's now five o'clock. I'll make us something to eat."

"I can't believe I slept that long. You don't have to make anything. I think it's about time I take care of you." She started to get up from the couch, and Mark instinctively reached out to help her up. Her legs were wobbly, and he immediately put his arm around her waist.

"I think I tried to get up too fast." Lacey could not explain the warmth that radiated through her body from Mark's tender touch. She was getting used to his tenderness. *Am I relying too much on this handsome man?* Tomorrow was her OBGYN appointment. *Should I ask Mark to go with me?* She thought perhaps that was too much to expect of him.

Their evening together was relatively quiet; they ate together and then watched TV for a short time. Mark finally asked if she would mind if he went downstairs to watch a game. I will check on you but if you want to go upstairs earlier, give me a holler. Lacey gave him a nod. Mark had put his TV, couch, and recliner downstairs. It was a finished basement but had been void of any furnishings. It was a great place for Mark when he wanted to give Lacey some space.

Lacey realized that Mark was quite the sports fan. He watched football, basketball, hockey, and when baseball was on, he watched as many games as possible. Yes, he was a big sports fan. She knew Dan did not share that same affinity for so many sports; he liked climbing. Climbing, she wondered, what was going to come of the so-called investigation? Lacey could not believe that anything so nefarious could have taken place and she shuttered at the thought.

It was getting late, and Lacey wanted to go to bed before she fell asleep on the couch again. Should she call for Mark or walk up the flight of stairs by herself. Hopefully she would get the "all clear" from the doctor tomorrow, so what was one more day? She started to get up when Mark came into the family room. "Lacey, are you ready to go up to bed?"

How did he know what I was thinking? "Yes, I thought I could do this on my own."

"Nope. I know it's one more day but let's just wait and see what the ultrasound shows and what doctor McDonald says tomorrow."

"Um, Mark, are you planning to go with me to the doctor tomorrow?"

"Yes, I thought I would. Unless you would rather not have me there." Lacey saw the disappointment in his eyes immediately. There was no way she could tell him that he did not have to go with her.

"No, that's fine. I would really like for you to come with me." She didn't miss how pleased he looked. *Well, I have told him this is our baby, not just mine.*

He picked her up in one swift swoop. He loved the way her arms always circled around his neck unconsciously as he drew her close to his chest. Yes, he would miss carrying her up and down the stairs.

They arrived at the doctor's office on time, however, it was not unusual to have to wait. It was obvious to Mark that Lacey was nervous; it was sketched on her face. Mark took her hand and held it in his lap. She didn't pull away but allowed him to hold it. Her hand felt cold and clammy, a sure sign of how nervous she was. "Lacey, the baby is fine and you're going to be fine. Haven't we been praying for this ultrasound?" It became as easy as tying a pair of shoes for Mark to pray before they ate, and he started to pray with Lacey before she went to bed. He prayed fervently for her and their baby. It always warmed his heart to know that she considered her precious baby girl to also be his. She nodded, however, he saw how her eyes glistened with unshed tears.

When Lacey was called back, she stood up and did not let go of Mark's hand. He was uncertain if she would want him in the exam room with her. Now he was just as nervous as she. He followed her into the room. The nurse had her up on the table asking if Lacey was ready to see

CHAPTER 14

her baby. He noticed her give a warm but shaky smile. "Yes, ready as we'll ever be." Mark was standing in the corner, unsure as to where exactly he should stand. He wanted to give Lacey all the privacy he could. He looked at everything in the room except at the nurse and Lacey.

"Okay, my dear. Let's get your slacks down low enough so we can get a good picture of your baby. Daddy, why don't you come on over so you can get a look at your little girl."

Mark could not believe that Lacey reached out her hand for him to take. She held on so tight he thought she would close off the circulation to his entire arm. Mark rubbed his thumb across the top of her hand. The gel was smeared on her abdomen and the ultrasound wand was placed on top of her bulging stomach. He hoped Lacey didn't see how huge his eyes must have gotten. He had no idea how big her stomach had become. *Well, she was seven months along, just two more to go.*

Soon the image was on the monitor. "There's your little girl. She's an active little thing so that's good." She began to point out her arms and legs, her little mouth, eyes, and her very strong heartbeat. "Honey, your baby is perfect. Her heart is strong; there is no sign of any stress. Nothing that has pulled away. She is still completely protected. I'll have Dr. McDonald come in and take a look."

The nurse left and it was just the two of them in the room. Lacey had huge tears streaming down her cheeks. "Sweetheart, are you okay?" Again, Mark called her sweetheart, unaware the words simply flowed out.

"Mark, I'm so overwhelmed. She's fine. Our little girl is fine. These are happy tears."

Without even thinking, Mark leaned down and gave Lacey the sweetest kiss. It wasn't passionate or demanding; it simply gave Lacey a feeling of peace and love. *Could Mark actually love her? Or was he only showing compassion for the situation she was in? No, I cannot believe that someone like Mark would ever love me in an intimate way. She had been married to his best friend. Oh, I know he loves me as a dear friend, and I have to be content with that.*

Dr. McDonald walked in right when Mark was wiping her eyes with a tissue. His smile was warm and caring. He knew of Lacey's situation and had met Mark at the hospital. After his greeting, he picked up the ultrasound wand. "Well, young lady, let's have a look, shall we?" The nurse had also come in with the doctor. She was anxious for the doctor to confirm what she had seen on the monitor and relieved she was not disappointed. "Everything is perfect. Your little girl is strong, and I'm sure anxious to meet her momma and daddy." He looked at Mark and gave him a knowing wink. Mark thought his heart would bust right out of his chest. This wasn't his flesh and blood baby, but he already loved her as if she were.

"Dr. McDonald, can I start going up and down the stairs? I have been so careful. Mark has been so patient in carrying me. I can't believe his back hasn't been killing him. I'm not exactly a lightweight now."

All four chuckled and secretly, Mark, was hoping the doctor would tell her it wouldn't hurt for him to continue carrying her. "Nope, all is good. You could even start running if that's what you have been used to. I'll see you next month, and then during your final month, I'll be seeing you every week until this little one comes. You need to think about the Lamaze classes at the hospital. I'm sure Mark will make an excellent coach for you."

"To be honest, I have not thought about the class. I will make sure we're signed up. Thanks Dr. McDonald."

Lacey was beaming when they walked out of the office. It was lunch time and Mark suggested he take her out to eat. She knew they had leftovers at home from all the meals they were given but going out sounded wonderful. "Mark, I would love going out for lunch. And if there's a ton of stairs, that's fine by me." Mark put his arm around her as they walked to his car. Nothing could keep her from the happiness she felt.

As they sat together at the table, Lacey wondered how to broach the subject of the Lamaze classes. *Oh, well, I might as well come right out and ask him. He can always refuse.* "Mark, how do you feel about attending

CHAPTER 14

the classes with me?" She wondered if he would even want to go. "I don't want to put you on the spot."

"Lacey, I would be honored to attend the classes with you. Just tell me when and where and I'll be there."

Chapter 15

After their lunch at Olive Garden, Lacey continued to feel like she was on cloud nine. All was right with her world. She was so happy ... until she walked into their home. Mark was the first to notice that the arcadia door, leading to the patio off of the family room, was open. He told Lacey to sit down at the kitchen table and not go anywhere. "Mark, what is it?"

"It may be nothing, but I don't believe either of us would have left the door open in the family room." Lacey shook her head, shocked to hear what Mark was saying.

"Do you think someone broke into our house?"

"You stay here while I take a look around. If anything is out of place, I'll have to call the police. I'm just thankful we weren't home." He saw the shock in Lacey's eyes. "Everything will be okay. I have to admit, I'm happy Detective Malone will be here tomorrow."

Mark left the sliding door untouched, just in case there were fingerprints. He looked in every room downstairs, went to the basement, and checked everything there ... nothing out of place. He went up the stairs but stopped short when he looked in his room. His drawers were opened; clothes lay on the floor in a heap. He walked to the bathroom; drawers were opened but nothing pulled out. He checked every room on his way to Lacey's master bedroom—shocked to see it a complete mess. Clothes were everywhere. Dan's drawers were pulled open; Lacey had cleaned out all of Dan's drawers. It was obvious that someone was angry, as each of Dan's armoire drawers were pulled out completely. First, he needed to call the police. After he reported the break-in, he went downstairs to Lacey.

"Lacey, I'm afraid you have to come upstairs. Your bedroom's a mess, and I have no idea what anyone could be looking for. I've called the police, and they're sending a detective over."

Lacey could only gasp, covering her mouth as she peered into her room. She looked horror stricken. Her dresser drawers emptied, even her desk lay toppled on the floor. Whoever it was, was looking for something… but what? She cautiously walked into the bathroom. Her vanity drawers were opened but nothing pulled out. The closet was a different story. It was a huge mess; all the storage bins and shoe boxes were ripped open and everything was piled in a heap on the closet floor. The two nightstand drawers were pulled out. "Mark, I don't understand. I can't imagine what anyone could be looking for. The only thing of value is Dan's Rolex—and of course, the Bible you gave him."

"Mark, what would they possibly be looking for in your room?" She left her room and proceeded to walk to his, shocked to see the mess. "Why? Why? I don't understand why anyone would do such a thing. Mark, could it be Judge Cramson? But what are they looking for?"

Mark immediately was at her side and wrapped his arms around her shoulders. *God, I don't know if she can handle much more. She has been through so much.* He drew her into a warm embrace. He felt her tremble as he ran his hands up and down her back. Her eyes were swimming in a pool of tears; the dam ready to burst. "Shush, honey, we're in this together. You're not alone." His words were comforting, however, the question remained… why?

They returned to Lacey's room, careful not to touch a thing as they waited for the police to arrive. Dan's watch was laying on the floor along with the Bible. Did the intruder know just how valuable that watch was? Lacey was sure whoever it was, was not interested in any of her possessions. No, they were looking for something specific … but what?

CHAPTER 15

When the police arrived, Mark took over and for this Lacey was grateful. They had a fingerprint specialist there, and he immediately got to work lifting what prints he could. The officer took both their statements, surprised that nothing, that they were aware of, was taken. This was not a routine break-in. The Rolex and Lacey's jewelry would have been taken. No, this looked like something far more nefarious. Nothing was out of place downstairs; the other two bedrooms upstairs were left untouched; however, their bedrooms were a different story. A few eyebrows were raised when Mark mentioned he had a separate bedroom. He shrugged and told the officer it was complicated. The officer simply nodded as if it was none of his business.

With Lacey's bedroom such a huge mess, Mark suggested he sleep in the extra bedroom. "Since my bed is a queen, you can sleep in my room, and I'll take the single bed in the other room."

"Absolutely not. That bed is way too small for you. Your feet will be hanging over the bed. No, I'll take the single bed." She chuckled at that announcement.

"Okay, but I don't want you walking around in your room. You have no idea what's on the floor until we start to clean up, and I don't want to touch anything until Malone gets here."

"I understand. I'll only grab what I need for the night. Your bathroom isn't as bad as mine. If you don't mind me using yours."

"Of course, I don't mind. In fact, tell me what you need, and I'll get it for you. I don't want you walking in your room with it in such shambles." By now it was dark, and Mark did not know what she could be walking in if she wasn't careful. It looked like shards of glass glistened in the carpet.

Detective Malone pulled up to the house the following afternoon. He was a handsome man in his early sixties. Mark met Malone when he picked him up at JFK in New York over three years ago. Malone had been hired by the Edwards brothers to find a missing person, who happened to be his sister. Other than the drive from and back to the airport, to pick up his sister at Jason Edwards's condo, Mark didn't have too much contact with him. He knew how impressed his brother-in-law, Jason, and his brother, Doug, were with Malone's detective skills. He only hoped he would prove himself capable of handling this. Getting to the bottom of Cramson's actions was far more convoluted than a missing person—at least in his mind.

Lacey's eyes looked hollow that morning as she sat at the breakfast table. Mark knew the break-in yesterday left her totally unnerved; it was understandable. "Lacey, Detective Malone just pulled into the drive." She simply gave him a nod. "Honey, I know Malone is a great detective, but let's remember, our hope and trust is in God."

"I know, Mark. Thanks for reminding me." *His names of endearment meant so much to her—but did he really mean them to be?*

Mark opened the door and greeted the detective. Mark brought Malone into the living room and introduced him to Lacey. His eyes were warm and friendly and immediately Lacey felt at ease. He agreed to a cup of coffee Mark offered as he took the seat opposite Lacey. "Mrs. Hamilton, I hope you don't mind answering some backstory questions. Jason Edwards filled me in on your current situation. I'm sure you and your husband have more details to offer."

"Yes, of course. I'm willing to answer any questions you have for me." Mark entered the living room with a coffee mug for Malone and a cup of tea for Lacey. He returned to the kitchen for his coffee.

Mark was pleased to see Lacey perfectly at ease as she answered several questions. Malone was taken aback when Lacey told him how she had never been accepted into the family. Hearing her confession caused Mark's heart to ache. *It had to be difficult knowing you were never accepted or good enough for the man you married. She was never loved by Dan's family much less liked by them.* Since Mark had taken

CHAPTER 15

a seat next to Lacey on the couch, he reached over and took her hand. Her smile was warm as she looked up at him. His touch strong yet gentle.

With Malone taking copious notes, he closed his notebook and said he wanted to look into both the Cramson's history. He acknowledged it may be difficult since one was a state superior court judge and the other a state prosecutor. "Don't look so discouraged, it may take a while, but I never stop digging." He told them he was staying at the Extended Stay Inn in Arlington, and to call him if they had any questions at all. He gave Mark his business card with his personal cell phone number. "If anything comes up, I will be sure to fill you in. I like to keep close contact with my clients." After a tour of the upstairs and seeing all the destruction, they all shook hands and Detective Malone left.

They never realized how late it was. "I can't believe he was here for over three hours." Lacey was stunned that he had so many questions. He went through every room in the house and came up with nothing; it was bizarre—nothing was touched downstairs; not even out of place. Other than the arcadia door being the point of entry.

"You did great, Lace. You were very thorough in all your answers. Malone also thinks the break-in was really to scare us."

"Yes. Unless—never mind."

"No. Tell me. Unless what?"

"Unless Judge Cramson thinks I have something he wants—though, I can't imagine what it could be."

Mark took one look at Lacey and saw the tiredness in her eyes. She looked exhausted. He walked over and took both her hands in his. "Lacey, why don't you lay down for a while. I'll start putting things together upstairs." Just then, she completely broke down and fell into his arms. Mark held her tight to his chest, rubbing her back to try and comfort her. "Babe, it's going to be all right. You have been through so much. What can I do to help you?"

Her body shook and with trembling voice she responded to Mark's offer, "Just hold me, Mark. Please, just hold me." He did not have to be told twice. He directed her to the couch and instinctively held her in his arms. Her head rested on his shoulder, and her arm wrapped around his waist. *Forever would not be long enough to hold her like this.* He kissed the top of her head as she snuggled as close to him as possible. Her sobs began to quiet and with that she began to hiccup. Soon even they stopped. He knew she had fallen asleep, but he was not about to let her go. Mark had no idea how long he sat with Lacey on the couch, but he awoke to complete darkness. He was stretched out on the couch with Lacey almost on top of him, still sound asleep on his chest. Oh, how he loved her, his heart ached at the thought. He wanted her more than his next breath. The thought of being a father in a couple of months gave him pause. *Lord, help me to be the best dad possible. I know I can't do it without you. The best dad and the best husband for Lacey.*

He readjusted Lacey. Her baby tummy made it impossible for her to lay right on top of him, but he needed her to be more on the couch so he fitted her between him and the couch. Suddenly, he felt the baby kicking into his stomach. It brought a chuckle that he tried to swallow. Lacey's eyes fluttered open. She looked up into Mark's eyes that were focused on her. She loved seeing his messed-up hair and his stubbly beard. "Oh, dear. I'm so sorry. I must have fallen asleep on you, Mark." She noticed his huge grin. "And what are you laughing about?" She looked adorable as Mark looked down on her. Just then, she realized the position she was in. "I'm so sorry, Mark. I must have fallen asleep and on you, no less."

"Hey, nothing to be sorry about. I was chuckling because our little girl decided to give me a swift kick in the stomach. I don't think she liked the position her momma was in."

Lacey could not help but smile up at him. "She definitely knows what she likes and does not like already." She loved that Mark said our daughter; it warmed her heart. She lay in his arms and he continued to stroke her back. She felt loved. *But could he really love her one day?* "We better get upstairs and clean up the mess."

"No, Lacey. I'm going to fix us something to eat. We'll clean up the mess tomorrow." After they ate, Mark went upstairs and cleared a path in Lacey's room so she could walk without stepping on anything. "Please be careful and only walk to your bed. There's a lot of broken glass."

Lacey heard the knock on her door. She had slept so soundly, however, looking around her room, the mess was still there. "Come in."

Mark cautiously entered her room. "Lace, how about some breakfast before we tackle all of this?"

Lacey was pleasantly surprised to see that Mark had breakfast ready when she came downstairs. "Mark, how sweet. Thank you so much. And I'm starved."

"Well, I figured we would need our strength to tackle the mess we have upstairs." He gave her a heart-warming wink. Lacey appreciated his jocular expression at such a serious time. "At least the downstairs was untouched, and it looks like it is only my room and yours."

"Yes, and that's the puzzle."

Mark reached for her hand and brought her to the table. "Come sit down and eat. Everything always looks better on a full stomach."

With full stomachs, they were both ready to tackle the mess upstairs. "Should we work together, or tackle are own rooms?" Mark was not sure if Lacey would want him going through her things.

"Why don't we work together. Perhaps with four eyes searching, we just might find some sort of clue."

"That sounds good to me, and since my room has the least in it, we can start there."

They worked together in silence as clothing and personal items of Mark's were put back in drawers, hung in the closet, or pictures and other items placed on his dresser and nightstand. For some reason, Lacey was getting a glimpse into Mark's personal life ... especially the pictures. He certainly loved his family. He had pictures of his sister and him when they were quite young, standing with his mom and the man that must have been his dad—one with just his sister and mom, and another with his sister and brother-in-law, Jason. Sweet pictures of him holding his nephew and yet another with his niece, Anna Beth, when she was a newborn. Her heart constricted seeing what an amazing family he had when she had no one. She felt the tears begin to slide down her cheeks, quickly wiping them away with the back of her hand. *It must be the silly hormones.* She stiffened when she felt Mark's strong arms around her, melting when she turned into his chest. "I'm so sorry. It must be my crazy hormones."

"Hey, that's okay. It's been a stressful time. Anything else going on that you want to talk about?"

"I'm fine." Her breath hitched a little. "Mark, you have an amazing family. I can't imagine having as many people in my life as you have."

"Is that why the tears?" He felt a little nod as she continued to lay on his chest. "Well, they're your family now too." He lifted her face to look at him. "Do you understand what I'm telling you? Every person in all those pictures is now your family. They're not just my family."

"If you only knew how much I had longed for a family. After my parents died, I literally had no one. Thank you for sharing your family with me."

"I'm not sharing ... they're as much yours as mine. Please accept that." She nodded and hugged him as tightly as she could with this huge beachball between them. Just then they both felt a kick. "Oh. Oh. There she goes!" Mark chuckled and gave her a quick peck on the top of her head. "Let's get back to cleaning up." With that said, Lacey pulled away from his embrace, and Mark immediately felt the loss.

Once everything was in order in Mark's room, and before they moved onto Lacey's, Mark had a burning question to ask her. "Lacey, do you want to tell me about your parents? I know they were both taken from you in an auto accident. What were they like?"

"Oh, Mark, my parents were wonderful." A tear began to slip down her cheek once again.

CHAPTER 15

"Hey, you don't have to talk about it if you would rather not. The last thing I want is to upset you."

"No, Mark, I think it's probably good that I do. I have never talked to anyone about my childhood and my parents. I was an only child, not because my parents wanted it that way though. You see, I was adopted since they could not have any natural children. They adopted me when I was an infant. To me they were the only parents I ever knew or needed. I loved them so much." She sniffed, not allowing any more tears. "Of course, you could say I was spoiled and extremely protected. I had a father who would have given me the moon if he could." Her voice sounded distant as if she were thinking of her parents and her growing up years. She brushed away the few remaining tears that glistened on her cheeks.

"Did you ever want to find your biological parents?"

"Not really. I guess the thought of someone wanting me would have been nice, but I tried not to think about it too much. My mom and dad were my natural parents as far as I was concerned. I never lacked for love from either of my parents. They planned on sending me to college although I have no idea how they planned to pay for four years of college, even at a state university. But I know that was their dream for me. Ready to tackle my room?"

Mark noticed the abrupt change in subject. Her parents meant the world to her and now she was alone. *Well, she has me now.* "Sure, and yours is a much bigger mess. Lacey, careful. Don't walk here—there's glass all over." She cautiously walked as far from the mess as possible. The one and only picture she had of her parents lay broken and in shards on the floor. Also, the wedding picture of Dan and her lay crushed as well. Instinctively, she fell to her knees. The tears once again were on the verge of spilling out.

"Lacey, the pictures look fine. All we need are a couple of new frames, and they'll be perfect." She nodded but the words seemed to be lodged in her throat. Her head knew they would be fine, but her heart felt just as broken as the frames. She watched helpless as Mark carefully picked up all the glass. "I'll get the rest vacuumed, but I suggest you always wear slippers or shoes when in here. Eventually it will all come up but better safe than sorry. It's good that you don't have shag carpet in here." What would she do without Mark? He was always looking out for her.

With all the glass picked up and the carpet vacuumed, they were ready to tackle everything strewn all over the floor. The closet was a complete mess as well. *What in the world could someone be looking for?* This was the million-dollar question Lacey struggled with. She started to pick up some of her clothes when Mark stopped her. "Let's have some lunch. You need to eat."

"But we just started!"

"Look at the time; it's two o'clock already. Don't forget you're eating for two. Let's eat and then get back to work." Lacey had found out that you didn't argue with Mark. *It must be the lawyer in him.* She acquiesced to his request—he didn't give her much chance to refuse as he grabbed her hand and pulled her up from the floor. "All this isn't going anywhere." He waved his arms at the clothes strewn everywhere. "After we have a bite to eat, we'll be in better shape to work on putting everything away. Look at it this way, your closet and drawers will be all cleaned out and perfect." The twinkle in his eyes was hard not to miss—they were full of mischief.

"You're right. And now that you mentioned food, I guess I could eat something." Just then a growl escaped, bringing laughter to the both of them.

After lunch, they worked side-by-side folding clothes, hanging up clothes, even discarding some. Mark could not help but notice that Lacey did not have all that many clothes. Suddenly, he heard her fall to the floor. Her body began to quake. *What in the world?* Mark was all set to run to her but noticed she sat with her and Dan's wedding rings in her hand. It was obvious that the small glass jewelry box lay broken on the floor. He could hear her soft sobs—it was gut wrenching. *What should I do? Go to her or give her time to grieve.* Since he had been working in the closet, hanging up clothes, he thought perhaps it best that he allowed

CHAPTER 15

her to have this time of privacy. He wished he had seen the rings on the floor and had picked everything up himself. He felt a sudden tightness in his chest, and his stomach clenched. *What is going on with me?* To his shock, he realized this feeling was jealousy. *"I've never been jealous in my life. How can I be jealous of a dead person, and my best friend?"* He wondered how he could go on once the baby came. *God, please remove any jealousy I have in my heart. I never felt this before, and I certainly can't live with something like this taking residence in my heart.*

He walked back into the room when he heard her begin to get up. "Hey, are you okay?" *What a dumb question. Of course, she wasn't okay.* She looked a mess, a beautiful mess. Just then it hit him that he could never replace Dan and the love she had for him. If she wanted to end their marriage after the baby was born, he would have to walk away.

Lacey simply nodded her head and set the rings on the dresser. She turned to find Mark standing right behind her, and without any hesitation she fell into his arms. The tears began to flow once again. "Everything will be okay, Lacey. I'm so sorry you have to go through all this. I wish I could take some of this pain away. One good thing, with Detective Malone on the case, I'm sure he will get to the bottom of this." He stroked her back as he held her close.

"Mark, I don't understand why you are so good to me. I have been nothing but a problem for you."

Oh, how he wanted to tell her that he loved her more than life itself. She and the baby had become his everything.

Lacey felt so secure and protected in his arms. She felt cherished and loved every time he held her like this. *And he wishes to take some of my pain? Who is like this?* "Thank you so much, Mark. I don't know what I would do without you."

They worked non-stop for over an hour. They worked their way to the overturned nightstand. The Bible Mark had given Dan lay on the floor along with his Rolex watch, some cufflinks, golf tees, even a couple of golf balls. They both had to chuckle at that. "Golf ball and tees? Who keeps these in a nightstand?" Lacey just shook her head as she continued to laugh at what they found.

When Lacey picked up Dan's Bible, a piece of paper that had been wedged into the spine, poked out. "Mark, was this your note?" Lacey knew it had been Mark's Bible.

He examined the note carefully. "No, this isn't mine."

"What does this mean? *I know what's going on* and then this number?"

Mark looked at Lacey. He was as confused as she was. "I have no idea. Where could Dan have gone after he left the office?"

"I didn't expect him home early. He called and said there was something he had to do. I just figured he was getting things together for his climb which was not unusual."

"Do you remember when he got home?" Lacey shook her head. "Even a guess."

"Probably around 8 or 8:30. Dinner was ready earlier, so he just grabbed a plate and sat at the TV and ate."

"Anything said where he went after work?"

"No, he did seem awfully quiet though. Then, before we went to bed, he said something amazing had happened to him at work and he would tell me all about it when he got home Saturday night. He seemed to perk up when he talked about sharing what happened at work. Now that I think about it, I can't remember him being that quiet before a climb. He was usually hyper and super excited about climbing."

"Did he talk to anyone before going to bed?" Lacey gave him an incredulous look. "I'm sorry, I don't mean to be the detective here."

"No, no, that's fine. I'm wondering where you are going with this."

"I'll give this note to Malone." The numbers were all run together; if it was a phone number, Mark wanted Malone to make the call. Mark took out his phone and gave Malone a call. Lacey sat motionless on the bed waiting for Mark to end the call. When he ended the call, he told Lacey that Detective Malone would stop by and pick up the note they found.

Chapter 16

Mark picked up the call that his secretary had put through. "Mark, oh my God, Mark." The sobs were uncontrollable, and he could barely make out who was calling.

"Lacey?"

"Oh, Mark. Mark, I need you!"

"Lacey, where are you? Are you okay? Is the baby okay?"

"Mark, I'm in jail!"

"Jail?! What are you talking about?! How can you be in jail?!"

"They've arrested me ... for the murder ... of my husband. Mark, what am I going to do?"

Lacey's sobs were beyond heart wrenching. He had never heard such agony. "Lacey, they can't do this. Tell me where you are and I'll be right down. And do not, I repeat, do not say a word to anyone. Tell them you need to wait for your attorney. Do you understand? You do not say a word without your attorney present." Lacey told him where they had taken her. He left the office in record time. He was sure he had beat his record when he got word that Lacey had been taken to the hospital. He called Malone as soon as he got in his car, pleased that he would be meeting him at the station.

Mark arrived at the station only to find his beautiful wife sitting in an interrogation room. It helped telling them he was her attorney. "Lacey, honey, tell me exactly what happened. Who arrested you?"

Her eyes were so swollen; she looked utterly drained and exhausted. She continued to sob as she tried relating the sequence of events to him. "Mark, they just forced their way into our home, and said I was under arrest for the murder of Daniel Cramson. Mark, where did that even come from?"

As they were talking, Detective Malone entered the room. Mark was surprised that they allowed him in, but then Malone had a way of getting around the authorities. Malone had worked for the NYPD as a detective for many years before retiring and going private.

"We must have really ruffled some feathers. He looked from Mark to Lacey. I think I got too close to something. Come on, we're getting out of here."

Lacey looked at him in disbelief. "You mean you and Mark? I don't think I can go anywhere." Now she was doing nothing but hiccupping.

"No, Lacey, we're all getting out of here. I know just who to talk to, and I don't think they're going to try anything like this again."

"But they arrested me for killing Dan!!"

"Let's get out of here and talk at home. We know you didn't do any such thing." Mark gave Malone a nod.

The officer came over and unlocked the cuffs they had on Lacey. She was handcuffed to the table that she sat behind. As soon as she was released, she fell into Mark's waiting arms.

"Come on, let's go. I've signed all the papers, so you're free to leave." She was stunned that Malone could do such a thing.

Lacey could not believe what just happened. All she had thought about all morning was being locked away and her baby being born in a prison hospital. She would never have a chance to even hold her. She shuddered at that thought. Her heart was beating out of her chest as they walked out of the jail. Mark held her so tight she thought he would squeeze the life out of her but she didn't care one bit. His arms felt so good.

When they returned home, Mark quickly made coffee for Malone and himself and a cup of tea for Lacey. They sat at the kitchen table in

CHAPTER 16

silence. When Mark sat down, his eyes focused immediately on Lacey's wrists. They were red from being locked in handcuffs. He reached over and gently rubbed her hands and wrists. "Lacey, I am so sorry I wasn't here when the police came."

"Mark, there's no way you would have known. I was in shock the way they forced their way in. They immediately grabbed me and put me in handcuffs."

"Did they read you your Miranda rights?" asked Malone.

"I don't think so but I honestly can't remember. I was in such shock. They took me out of the house and into the police car so quickly my head was spinning. Once I was in the back seat of the police car, I totally broke down. It hit me. Oh, Mark, all I could think of was our baby being born in a prison hospital and taken from me immediately. We would never get to see her much less hold her. Mark, I think I would die if that happened to me." Her lip began to tremble as she took a breath.

"Lacey, everything is okay; you're home now." Mark had moved next to her and wrapped her in his strong embrace—it felt so right. Mark knew he would have a talk with Malone to find out how he got her out so quickly. "I think Cramson thought that if he could get you convicted with the murder of Dan, that would give them an easy path to getting our baby girl." Man, he shuddered to think of just how evil the Cramsons were. "How could they be so relentless and evil in what they are willing to do?"

Detective Malone had to agree. "We are dealing with someone with a whole lot of power. I'm determined to get answers. I'm sure as soon as questions were being raised as to Dan's death not being an accident, we got too close to the fire."

"Yeah, but how would they even know this question had been raised? I only spoke to one of Dan's climbing buddies. I asked him not to say anything; not even to Steven the other friend that he climbed with."

"Do you think he kept it to himself?"

"I don't know. I did disclose the concern we had when I spoke to him on the phone. I only asked if Dan's gear had been checked out.

The next morning, I met with Jeremy. He said he had called Steven the night before. He would have liked meeting with us but had a business meeting out of town. After we talked, I asked him to keep our discussion to himself."

"That's interesting. Mrs. Hamilton, how well do you know the men your husband climbed with."

"Please, call me Lacey. I knew Jeremy and his wife fairly well. We had gone out to dinner together several times. Steven, I never met; he had only climbed with Jeremy and Dan for a couple of months, if that. Dan said that Steven seemed like a nice enough guy and was an expert climber. I don't believe they were close at all."

"Did you know his stepbrother went climbing with them?"

"No, I had no idea. I had never met his stepbrother. Excuse me. I need to use the restroom."

When Lacey left the room, Mark took this opportunity to open up with Malone. "She's not out of the woods, is she?"

"No. I don't think she is. Let's hope they never read her her rights. The prosecuting attorney is a Victoria Grilly."

"That's Mrs. Cramson. She goes by her maiden name in court."

"No kidding. That in itself is rather suspicious. I have to keep digging into the Cramsons and their determination to get Lacey's baby from her." Mark felt a twinge of hurt; she was their baby.

"You mean our baby. I'll fight with everything I have to keep Lacey and our baby safe."

"I'm sure you will."

"How were you able to get Lacey out of jail? I'm an attorney, and I know things don't usually work that quickly."

Malone gave a warm chuckle. "As soon as I walked up to the Captain's desk, he looked up and we recognized each other immediately. Turns out we worked together in the same New York precinct for years. He was a Lieutenant at that time. We always did get along, and I was disappointed to hear he had left NYPD for another position. I had no idea that he had left the state and became Captain here in Texas. Once

CHAPTER 16

I explained the circumstances, he released her immediately. They have no concrete evidence to hold her. The prosecuting attorney was the one that insisted on the warrant."

Mark was glad their conversation was over as Lacey reentered the kitchen. He did not want her to worry over what may happen if they did not discover the source of the Cramsons' hatred and why they were carrying this out to such an ugly extreme. Yes, he would protect his wife and child with every breath within him.

Malone picked up where he left off asking about Dan's stepbrother, Jude. Mark could tell him more than Lacey could. "Were you able to figure out the number on that note I gave you?"

"Believe it or not, I called the number. It was obviously a phone number, however, it was out of service. I have someone in New York working on identifying who that number belonged to. With that statement on the note, someone definitely knows what's going on."

"Do you have anything on the Cramsons?"

"Not yet. I also have someone digging into their background."

"Well, I hate to say this but I think it's obvious that his stepbrother had something to do with Dan's murder." Mark had already given this a lot of thought however, this was the first that he actually verbalized it. He heard Lacey gasp when he said this. He reached across the table and grabbed her hand. "We'll find out for sure, Lace. As an attorney, I shouldn't jump to any conclusion without all the facts. We will get all the facts." Mark looked at Malone, and he was thankful he saw confidence in Detective Malone's eyes.

Chapter 17

Malone sat on the couch in his hotel room. He was tired of pacing—anxious to hear something, anything at all from the guys working on the information he had given them. It was over a week now, and he couldn't imagine that they had found nothing. The police captain told him about the interview their detective had with Jude and Steven after talking to Jeremy. Steven was jumpy and a bit too unsettled for him but then, having a detective questioning you could make anyone jumpy. Jude was a different story entirely. He said he was calm but evasive in a lot of his answers and had acted as if someone was always looking over his shoulder. He would have his own interview with them.

He met the captain at the station once again and together they examined all of Dan's equipment. At first, everything looked kosher, and it didn't look like anything was tampered with. Until Malone let out a hoot. "Look at this will you. Look at the harness."

The captain came over and looked closely at it once again. "We never caught that before. Why, that isn't just frayed; you can actually see the cuts up higher ... here and here. Definitely cut with a sharp tool."

"Yeah, like a box cutter or really sharp blade of some sort. And it's only a few nicks but ..."

"Enough to weaken the whole harness. No one would even catch this at first glance." The captain looked as assured as Malone. "We're definitely looking at murder. What about the Cramsons or ... Hamilton's wife?"

"Not a chance. When I've talked to her, all I see is pain in her eyes. Nah, knowing them like I do and what she's been going through, no way would she have done this. And besides, she had nothing to gain—no life insurance money, no big savings, or investments, nothing. From what I have investigated, she was left with a mortgage and a lot of bills."

"Well, someone wants to frame her."

"Yes, but only since I started investigating the case. And, I have no idea who would have tipped the guilty party off. But I have a feeling they were before I even got here."

Malone met Mark at his office. He knew they could talk more openly. After a quick handshake, Mark asked what he could do for him. "I was over at the station and Captain Burk and I went over Dan's equipment."

"I thought you already did that and didn't find anything."

"We did. It was entirely different this time, and I can't believe we missed it the first time. I was ready to give up when I noticed some small but very sharp nicks in his harness. We were always looking at the frays. The frays were so distinguishable that it was too easy to believe that it was because of the age of the harness that it came apart. All it took was that one location and when it broke, it was made to look like stress." Malone could only shake his head. "Someone definitely knew what they were doing."

"So, where does that leave us?"

"It leaves us with a lot of questions. One being, who did you say you talked to before I came out here?"

"I got the names of Dan's climbing buddies from Lacey. I only spoke with Jeremy. I guess he mentioned it to Steven."

"What about the stepbrother? You had questions about him, right?"

"Yeah. I know they didn't have much in common, and I was shocked to hear he went climbing with them. I only met him a few times when we were at Harvard together and that was a long time ago. Lacey was totally unaware that he even had a stepbrother. He wasn't even at their wedding as far as I know."

"Tell me what you do know of him."

CHAPTER 17

Mark began to tell Malone how strange their dinners were at the Cramsons'. "It was obvious that Jude was favored by the Judge and Dan somewhat favored by the mom. It was also obvious that Dan didn't measure up to what they expected of him. I felt like they always compared him to me."

"Why the comparison?"

Mark was embarrassed to admit that he had straight A's and had spent a lot of time tutoring Dan. Mark shrugged his shoulders, "Dan made it to Harvard because of his parents and their connections and money; I made it on scholarships. It was still work."

Detective Malone realized he was talking to a very bright lawyer. "Now I understand how you made partner in such a short time." Mark nodded and thanked him for the compliment. "I talked to Jeremy and Steven, now I think I'll pay Jude a visit. I'll get back to you A.S.A.P."

"Thanks. I'd appreciate that."

When Mark arrived home, he was greeted by a very upbeat Lacey. It warmed his heart to see her so excited. "Hey, what's going on? You're certainly in a good mood. And something smells really good. What's for dinner?"

"I have a roast in the oven. It should be done in about a half hour. We'll have that with mashed potatoes and gravy. What would you like for a vegetable? I have carrots, broccoli, green beans, corn ... that's about it."

"Hey, I'll have whatever you want. But I need to know what has you in such a good mood."

"Well, you might not be as excited as I am, but I have us enrolled in the birthing classes at the hospital. They start next Monday. They're once a week for four weeks." She gave him a very sheepish look just then. "Do you still want to be my coach?"

"Absolutely. Just tell me where and when. It sounds like they'll end about a week before your due date."

"Yes. And being that close we won't forget anything." They both chuckled at that thought. "They're at the hospital where our baby will be born and where my doctor is; the class is at 5 p.m. I'm afraid you may have to leave work early to be there at 5. Is that going to be a problem?" She looked adorable as she stood anxiously biting her lower lip.

"Not at all. All my court cases are scheduled for morning, and they won't go past 1 or 2 o'clock, and sometimes the court even dismisses early." Mark was thrilled that Lacey would include him in this important event. He had to admit he had unexplained butterflies the moment she mentioned birthing classes; he planned on a quick call to his sister before the first class started. At least he had the weekend to prepare. *Nothing like knowing what you're getting yourself into. Then again, maybe the statement, ignorance is bliss, really meant something.* "Do I have time for a quick shower?"

"Of course. By the time I get the potatoes mashed and the gravy made, I'm sure you'll be done." One look at Mark, and Lacey knew what he was about to say. "And no, you are not going to mash the potatoes. Thanks anyway." If he ever wanted to lean down and kiss her, it was then. She looked adorable and better than he had seen her in a long time. She always looked like she carried the weight of the world on her shoulders. It was no wonder with all she had been through.

He wanted to be as upbeat and confident as Lacey, however, in the back of his mind, was the unspoken concern that Lacey was not out of the woods. Once Mrs. Cramson found out that Lacey had been released and there were no grounds to hold her, he was certain this woman would find something else to falsely convict her of. They had to get to the bottom of this before the other shoe dropped. He would put nothing past the Cramsons.

The next day Malone was finally going to meet with Jude. He had tried several times to reach him but always got his voice mail. He feared the man was avoiding him. Jude did not live with his parents, which he was pleased to see. He had his own apartment in a rather upscale

CHAPTER 17

neighborhood. He shook his hand as soon as he opened the door. Malone introduced himself and Jude invited him in. Malone thought he seemed a bit nervous but then most people were when he told them who he was. "What can I do for you Detective?"

"I'm sure you are aware that I'm investigating the death of Dan Cramson. I understand he was your stepbrother, correct?"

"Yes, he was. I have to tell you that his accident was quite a shock and something I will never forget."

"Did you climb with Dan often?" Malone wondered how forthcoming he would be. He knew he never climbed with him, but Jude didn't know this.

"No. Never." Droplets of sweat were forming on his forehead. He seemed awfully nervous and anxious—Malone wondered why the sudden change. "Dan called and asked if I wanted to join him that Saturday, and I told him it sounded like fun."

"And yet you had never climbed with him. Didn't it seem odd that he would call and invite you when you had never gone with him before?"

"Not at all. We were always pretty close growing up." His posture changed, and he shifted on the couch. Malone sat across from him in a barrel chair; completely cool and relaxed.

"So, you did a lot of things together growing up."

"Yeah, pretty much."

"What about as adults? Did you do much together?"

"The usual. Well, maybe we didn't do much together, but we talked on the phone a lot."

"So, when was the last time you talked to Dan?"

"I called him a few weeks ago. That's when he asked if I wanted to go climbing."

"I thought Dan called you."

"Oh, yeah, he did call me."

"How well do you know Jeremy and Steve?"

"Who?"

"The other two guys you were climbing with."

"Oh, yeah, them. I met them for the first time that morning. Hey, I already talked to the cops about this. I told them everything I know." Malone could not help but notice how jittery he became; he could almost see his heart pumping in his chest. Something suspicious was definitely at play here.

"Who do you think tampered with Dan's equipment?"

Jude looked startled that Malone would mention such a thing. "Ah, someone tampered with his equipment?" The detective simply nodded. "My guess, it was probably Dan's wife. She was only interested in his money."

"Is that right? What's her name again? Tracey, Sally?"

"Yeah, Tracey. I met her a few times. Like I said, she was really a gold digger. I knew the moment I met her she was after Dan's money."

It was obvious Jude had never met Lacey. "Well, I guess I had better give her a call." Jude nodded in agreement, looking relieved. This was getting more bizarre by the minute. "Okay then, I'll keep in touch. If there is anything at all that you can think of, give me a call." Malone reached in his shirt pocket and handed Jude his card; he knew there was no way he would ever hear from him. Something was not right: either Jude was the culprit, or he knew who was. The fact that he was willing to pin this on Lacey was the real question. *Why was he so quick to pin it on her? Lacey had been arrested for the murder of her husband. How would Jude even know about that?*

Malone left Jude's with more questions than answers. *If he would only come clean. Maybe he's protecting someone ... but who?* He was drained when he returned to his room. It was late enough to shower and hit the sheets. As he emptied his pockets, his phone buzzed. Hopefully, his guys in New York had the information he was looking for. "Malone here. Hey Jim, I sure hope you have some info for me."

Jim was a good friend who worked undercover for Malone. A true friend and someone he would trust with his very life. "Well, I was able to get the name of the person using that phone number you gave me. It was a throwaway and only used twice."

CHAPTER 17

"Okay." Malone waited with bated breath.

"The guy who used it is a Steven Grainer; he made one call to Jude Cramson, and it had one incoming from a private number that we're still trying to trace."

"Bingo. Thanks, Jim. Can you send me that info? I want the dates and time."

"Will do."

"Any word on the other matter?" He was hoping he had something on the Judge and his wife."

"Still digging. Right now, it doesn't look like the Judge is totally clean. As soon as I have anything, I'll let you know."

"Thanks. Call anytime."

"Will do. I have a couple of guys looking into the Judge and Mrs. Cramson."

"Sounds good." Malone waited until he got the phone info from Jim. He was anxious to know the time frame. *Was Jude the one who sliced the harness or Steve? One of them was guilty, or maybe both.* He received the date and times the phone was used, saved it and showered. This was a really big deal.

Chapter 18

Lacey sat anxiously waiting for Mark. She had arrived at the hospital at 4:30 and now it was 4:50. She feared Mark got tied up in a case, forgot about it, or worse yet, had changed his mind. *Maybe he decided this was not something he wanted to do. After all, what man would really want to be a coach for someone not carrying his own baby?* As soon as a couple of tears began to escape, she quickly wiped them away. Just then, she looked up to see Mark flying through the door. "Oh, Mark, you made it."

"Of course. I'm sorry if I'm late. I thought you said I needed to be here at 5."

"Yes, the class is at 5. I guess I got here a little early." Mark grabbed her hand and saw relief in her eyes. "I just ... oh, never mind."

"No, tell me."

"I was so afraid that you got tied up with a case or forgot."

"And what else?"

"I was afraid you changed your mind and didn't want to be my coach."

"Sweetheart, I would never change my mind about that. I'm so happy you asked me. And to be honest, I didn't get out any earlier because I called my sister to ask her what I could expect. To tell you the truth, I was a little apprehensive. I still am."

"Mark, I hope she helped. This is all totally new to me too." He could not help but take in just how adorable she looked. She had a maternity workout outfit on, and her beautiful auburn hair was pulled back in a high ponytail. A few tendrils had escaped and framed her face. She noticed how he looked at her and quickly said, "they said to dress comfortably. Is this too casual ... maybe not appropriate." At seven-and-a-half months, she was beginning to feel like a beached whale.

"You look perfect." He grabbed her hand as they made their way to the elevator and then up to the 5th floor. Her beautiful green eyes sparkled; it was good to see her so happy. They had no problem finding the room. There were about six other couples all milling about. The nurse holding the class was going about introducing herself to everyone. She noticed Mark and Lacey entering and was upon them immediately. Warmth spread through Mark's chest as Lacey introduced him as her husband. She did not make any other comments as to their relationship.

The coaches were instructed to take a seat in the low beanbag chairs on the floor. The moms-to-be sat in front leaning against their coach. Being held by Mark felt comforting as she lay cocooned against his chest. His incredibly broad chest, and strong arms wrapped around her were enough for her to lose all thought, to say nothing of how good he smelled. *He certainly has become my protector—and I'm afraid I'm falling in love with him. What? Did I just admit I'm falling in love with him?*

Time went by quickly and once the class was over, Mark suggested they go out for a bite to eat. Lacey wondered how to approach the subject, but she knew she had to say something and the last thing she wanted was for him to feel uncomfortable. "Mark, I really don't know how to say this, but I'm so sorry if you felt uncomfortable in the class."

"What? What are you talking about?"

"You know, when the instructor had us leaning against our coaches. I never realized how intimate that could be."

"Hey, don't even think about it. It was fine. I never gave it a thought." Now he knew he was lying to her. He had enjoyed every moment of it and wished he could hold her like that forever. She fit perfectly as she lay against his chest. Her hair was up in that adorable ponytail; but as she lay against his chest, she realized her ponytail was pressing into him. She quickly took out her clip and let her thick, beautiful hair flow well past

CHAPTER 18

her shoulders. He could not help but rub his nose in the sweet aroma ... *strawberries, or was it vanilla? I'm a guy, what do I know. Whatever it was, it was intoxicating.* Mark had all he could do to keep from running his fingers through it. He could handle the breathing, the support and the rubbing of her back, none of that was a problem. However, he had to admit that holding her close as she lay into him felt really good ... too good. Like she really did belong to him. He felt an overwhelming possessiveness that he didn't expect to feel. He thought this would be the easy class but holding her so close was torture.

When they returned home, Mark knew he had to unwind and release some of the tension that he continued to feel after that class. Yes, it was intimate, and he struggled with the thought of going through three more classes. Lacey went into the family room and kicked off her shoes. Her feet were starting to swell from her pregnancy. His first thought was to kneel in front of her and rub her feet but right now, he couldn't think straight. Instead, he told her he was going to cut the grass. He ran upstairs to change into jeans and a t-shirt and then flew out the door. Lacey could not help but wonder what she may have said or done to cause Mark to be so distant. It wasn't like him at all. She opened the book she had been reading while wondering if she should say something to Mark about his strange behavior.

By the time he came back in, he immediately ran up the stairs to shower. It seemed like a very long shower he was taking. When he came down, he stayed in the kitchen and asked if she would like some popcorn or some ice cream. *Was he avoiding her?* she wondered. "Ice cream sounds great. I can get it for us."

"No." He realized he sounded abrupt in his answer and corrected his tone. "I'm fine." He knew she liked chocolate syrup on her ice cream and a little whip cream. He made one for himself and brought them into the family room. As he handed her the bowl, he noticed sadness in her eyes. *Was it the hormones or something he said?* "Lacey, did I say something or do something to upset you tonight?" She shook her head but found it difficult to say anything. "Come on, I must have done something wrong."

She knew she had to say something, or it would bother her all night. "Mark, I thought maybe I said or did something to upset you. When we came home, you seemed to avoid me and left to cut the grass without saying much of anything. It's not like you to be so distant. I thought for sure I must have said or done something wrong."

"Oh, sweetheart, to be honest, and this is difficult for me to admit but I lied when I told you I was totally fine holding you in the class … the problem was, I was fine, more than fine. I should not have enjoyed it as much as I did." He ran his fingers through his thick hair, struggling as what to say next. The tension in the room evaporated at his confession. He knew he had to be honest with her, however, opening up his heart and his love for her was a bit more difficult. He hoped in time he could do this.

"Mark, I'm so sorry. If it made you uncomfortable, perhaps you should skip the next three classes."

"No, no way. I'm all in. I have to admit that it helped mowing the lawn." *And the cold shower, but he wouldn't tell her that.* She gave him the most sheepish and adorable smile. He quickly cleared his throat and changed the subject. "However, when it comes to watching the birthing videos the nurse talked about will be an entirely different story. Hopefully, I'll get through it without passing out." This caused a giggle to escape. "What's so funny? I really need to get my head wrapped around this whole thing." They ate their ice cream which by now was a little soupy but still tasted great.

Mark took Lacey's dish, however, before he got up, she took hold of his arm. "Mark, are we good? I mean, you know … good. I'm not making you feel uncomfortable."

"Lace, we're good. I just know I want to be there for you and the baby." He caught her sideways glance.

"Our baby, Mark. Don't forget she's our baby." His eyes glistened at her reminder.

Lacey still sat with her shoes off and feet resting on the ottoman. Without hesitation or thought, Mark took her feet and placed them in his

CHAPTER 18

lap. He began to massage her feet and she moaned in appreciation. "That feels so good, Mark. My feet are beginning to look like two huge sausages."

"You need to keep them up whenever possible. I think you're doing too much around the house. I've thought of hiring a cleaning service."

"What? I can certainly clean the house, Mark."

"For the most part, but I don't want you washing floors and vacuuming, especially when the baby's here, you'll definitely have your hands full ... me and the baby to take care of."

She swatted his arm. "Like you're so much work. You're the one that's been taking care of me. How quickly you forget."

"Sweetheart, I love taking care of you. You are not work." After he massaged both her feet, her eyes were half closed. "I think you better head up to bed." Teasingly he added, "you know, carrying you now might be a little much. I don't think my back could handle it." She immediately swatted his arm once again and told him how mean he was. She couldn't help but tickle him senseless. Before he could retaliate, she was up and running up the stairs to bed and hollered her goodnight over her shoulder. "Goodnight, Lacey." *I love you. I wish I could tell you that now. I would shout it from the rooftop.*

CHAPTER 19

Malone thoroughly enjoyed the breakfast buffet they served at the Extended Stay. The made-to-order omelet, fresh waffle with strawberries and whip cream were to die for. He was sure he had gained at least ten pounds in the two weeks he had been here. He was getting a little anxious to see this case come to a close. He had a couple of other jobs back in New York and had his capable team working on them, however, nothing like being hands-on himself. He still got antsy when he didn't have answers—he felt he was so close to solving this case. If the guys in New York that were working on this case, didn't come up with anything on the Judge and his wife, he would have to call it and that did not sit well with him. Without a doubt, he knew there was something unsettling … but what? He hated to leave with an unsolved murder.

As he sat with his notebook open and drinking his third cup of coffee, *I need to stop drinking so much of this stuff; that would be like cutting off a limb.* Just then his phone rang. "Malone here."

"Hey boss. I may have something I think is worth looking into."

"I hope it's good, I'm about ready to hang it up here. But I can't ignore the gut feeling I have."

"I finally found out who made the call to Steven. Drum roll please. It was the Judge himself. And you will be surprised what I found out about him and his dear wife."

"Okay. Spill it. My heart is really starting to pound."

"Our judge seems to have a huge gambling problem. He is in debt up his kazoo."

"Huh, no kidding."

"Yeah, the guy needs money to cover his you know what. But you said his son didn't have a huge insurance policy." Wait for this. He did have a huge policy … in Dan's name. The guy made the mistake of including any heirs. The money would go to Dan's heir, and if there was no heir, it would revert back to Judge Cramson and his wife."

"Well, I'll be. The guy was willing to knock off his son and any kids he had. How much is the policy?"

"I'm sure when he wrote the policy, there was no heir in sight. Get this, the policy is a whopping two million bucks. But he can't claim it because Dan's wife is pregnant and once, she has her baby, the money goes to Lacey and her child."

"So, Judge Cramson hired a hit man."

"It sure looks that way, Boss."

"It has to be Steven or Jude. If I can isolate one of them, I'm sure one will cop a plea and turn on the other one."

"Then, if we can get one to admit to being hired by Cramson—man, we need to get his gambling debts."

"I'm already on it. He goes by an alias, a Paul Grill."

Malone let out a whoop. "For a judge, he's not too bright. His wife's maiden name is Grilly." He couldn't hold back the laughter bubbling out of him. "Jim, we got him. Amazing work."

"I'll email what info I have on his debts. Most everything I could recover is there—where he gambled, even online gambling. All I had to do was follow the money."

"Good. Good. And send me the phone records on that disposable phone. I can't believe it. I was so close to hanging it all up and hoping Steven or Jude would come clean. I can't imagine how relieved that sweet couple will be. Mrs. Hamilton has been through so much."

"Everything I have is on the way."

CHAPTER 19

"Thanks, buddy. I'll submit what we have to the Dallas Police Department and the Texas AG. But first, I must visit the Hamilton's. Mr. Hamilton is a lawyer, and I'm sure when he sees this, he'll be looking at everything through the eyes of the law and what steps he may want to take. I'm sure he wants to see them locked up and perhaps file his own lawsuit against them." As he continued to talk, he saw all the info from Jim was coming through. "Thanks again for the good work. I'll keep you up to speed."

As everything came through, he was already on his way to the hotel's office to get all the documents printed. Then, he would be on his way to the Hamilton's. After that, a visit to the police department and then a visit with Jude Cramson. He was the most unsettled between he and Steven. If they could get him to crack, maybe both guys would turn state's evidence against the Judge and his wife. He knew they would be up against two power houses.

When Richard Malone got to the Hamilton's, he was greeted by Lacey and another attractive woman who he was introduced to. "Detective Malone, it's so good to see you." Agnes stood with her daughter-in-law looking very protective of her. "Detective Malone, this is my mother-in-law, Agnes Hamilton. She has come for a visit. May I help you with anything? Mark should be home any time now."

"Nice to meet you Mrs. Hamilton. The information I have, I would like to share with the both of you. Do you mind if I sit and wait for your husband?"

"No, please sit down." After asking, Lacey's mother-in-law quickly excused herself to serve them coffee and cookies that she had baked in the morning.

Agnes wondered why she suddenly felt so flustered, other than the detective was a very handsome older gentleman. She then realized that he was the detective that had found her daughter, Jessie. She thought his name sounded familiar. She had never met him before but knew the important part he played in trying to locate her daughter who had suffered serious memory loss after a horrific automobile accident in the mountains. She had to smile at the remembrance, because it was the tragedy that brought Jason and Jessie together.

As she walked into the living room with the tray, Malone was up immediately and took it from her. She was sure she must have turned a very deep pink. It had been a long time since a man caught her fancy, and he was not only handsome but a real gentleman. "Thank you, Mr. Malone."

He cleared his throat, "call me Richard or Rick, Mrs. Hamilton."

"Well, I guess you could call me Agnes then." Lacey sat taking it all in; it was cute to watch. Of course, she knew her mother-in-law was a widow; however, she had no idea of Malone's marital status. Her antennae had gone up. She would never allow Agnes to be hurt in any way.

As they were enjoying their coffee and cookies, Mark came in and was surprised to see the detective there. He warmly greeted him, hoping desperately he had any news at all regarding the investigation. "Good to see you, Detective. I sure hope you have some good news for us."

Malone started to unfold all the information that Jim had uncovered. He handed all the printed documents to Mark. Both Mark and Lacey sat in awe. This was way more than what they expected. "Wow, this is amazing," said Mark. He took one look at his wife and saw the tears streaming down her face. He was at her side immediately. As he embraced her, he felt her trembling. "Sweetheart, this is the best news we could have heard."

"I know Mark and I have tears of grief and of joy. I can't imagine his parents could have been so cruel and greedy to actually kill their own son. What parent would do that?"

"People who have no concept of what a relationship to Jesus Christ is. It shows the evil that can be in the heart of man when greed and sin take hold. They were desperate to pay his gambling debt. No doubt he was threatened with his life or blackmailed. As a judge, he would be removed from the bench if exposed."

CHAPTER 19

Mark sat with Malone for a long time discussing the steps they would be taking. Mark told him of his friend Judge Larsen who had married them. "I know I can trust him and get some sound advice as to how to proceed."

"You being an attorney, you may want to consider your own lawsuit against them."

"What good would that do, unless it can convince the court. I think Lacey and I just want to see them put away for a very long time."

"Well, I'm heading over to the Dallas Police Department. I think the Captain and I have some work to do. You contact Judge Larsen. We need this to go to the AG of Texas. I'm sure the Cramsons are going to fight us all the way."

"Not if we can get Jude or Steven to admit who initiated this--the Judge, his wife, or both. Either way, it looks like they were in it together." Detective Malone stood to leave; he walked over to Agnes and unashamedly took her hand. "Agnes, it was very nice meeting you."

"Thank you. It was very nice meeting you as well, Rick." Both Lacey and Mark noticed the blush. Was that a sparkle in his mom's eye?

When Malone had left, Mark looked at his mom and chuckled. "What's so funny, Mark? Do you think I'm too old to turn a head?"

"No, Mom. Not at all."

Lacey chimed in, "we don't know if he's single or not, do we?"

"He's single. I think he's a widower. Jessie and Jason would know more about him. But Mom, don't get any ideas."

His mom swatted him on the arm. "Oh, Honey. I'm too old to think about romance."

Mark pulled his wife and mom to his side. "I think we need to give thanks for what we heard today. God definitely has done more than we could have hoped for or expected." Mark led the three in prayer, and there wasn't a dry eye among the three of them.

Richard Malone strode into the station on a mission. He was certain his friend, the captain, was an honest man. Malone presented all the information to the captain. "Amazing work, Malone. You nailed it. Who do you want to talk to first, Steven or Jude?"

"I've thought about it. Jude was the most nervous one. Can you do a background check on Steven? I wouldn't be surprised if he's been in trouble before."

"We'll get on it right away."

"I would appreciate if this were kept between the two of us. Call it instinct but with the Cramsons' power, we can't trust anyone ... even in your police department." The captain looked aghast at his comment, then conceded. "You're right. Someone as powerful as the Judge, even his wife, as a lead prosecutor, can buy a lot of influence. Let's pay a visit to Jude. I'll do the background check on Steven myself when I get back." Malone gave him a nod and patted him on the back.

The captain grabbed his jacket and hat. Before he put his jacket on, he shouldered his weapon. "Better to be prepared." Malone was never without his—holstered on his leg.

Jude answered his door on the third knock. The two men wondered what could have taken him so long. His condo wasn't that large from what Malone remembered. As soon as he opened the door, Captain O'Malley flipped open his badge and asked if they could come in. "Yes, of course. He shook hands with the captain and then Malone. "Detective Malone, is that correct?"

"Yep. You remembered. I'm impressed."

"Well, what can I do for you? As you can see, I'm pretty busy and was getting ready to leave. I have some important business to take care of."

"We won't keep you long. A few questions, that's all." Together they eyed his suitcase that sat at his bedroom door. Malone gave O'Malley a nod. They both observed the obvious; he was leaving the country. "Jude Cramson, you are under arrest for the murder of Daniel Cramson. You have the right to remain silent. Anything you say can and will be used against you in a court of law." O'Malley read him his complete Miranda rights as he handcuffed him."

"You can't do this. Do you have any idea who my parents are?"

CHAPTER 19

"Yes, we do."

"Hey, it wasn't me. I had nothing to do with cutting his harness."

Malone and O'Malley exchanged looks; this was going to be easier than they thought. "Let's take a ride."

"I want to talk to my attorney."

"Not a problem. You can make that phone call when we get to the station." No doubt he would be calling his mother.

Malone wondered if his mother would throw him under the bus and let him rot in jail for the murder of his own brother. Something he was sure of; she and her husband were the real perpetrators.

Jude sang like a bird after he met with his mom. She was going to put all the blame on both him and Steven. It turned out that all Jude did was get Dan's equipment, which he kept in his parents' garage. He confessed to ransacking the Hamilton's house. Admitted he was looking for the paper he had given Dan. Once the murder was committed, he knew the number would incriminate all of them. He said he was angry when he couldn't find the note, and thought it would throw everyone off if they thought it was merely teenagers doing the destruction. He gave the equipment to Steven who very carefully cut the harness. Jude said he couldn't believe Steven was willing to go to prison for five-grand. Of course, he was promised another ten when the job was completed, and that's how they got the Judge and his wife.

After talking to Steven, a sting operation was set up for him to meet with Judge Cramson for the additional ten thousand. He met them at a restaurant not far from the Cramsons' home. Amazing what a little pressure can do when a guy tells you he will go to the cops and confess everything if he didn't get paid. Malone and Captain O'Malley were already seated at a booth when the Judge and his wife came in. They were seated at the booth across from them. It wasn't long before Steven came in; it was obvious he knew who to look for. The Cramsons' did not know that Steven was wearing a wire. Steven started talking, asking where the rest of his money was.

"We had an agreement remember. Five and then ten when the job was completed. Well, I completed the job. You also had me run that Hamilton woman off the road. I know you wanted her killed, or at least lose her baby." Malone and O'Malley looked at each other with a nod.

"You certainly botched that job. She and her baby lived. My boy, do you think I have ten-grand on me? Why don't we go for a little ride to my house? It's not far from here."

"Nah, ah. You give it to me now or I go right to the cops."

"I'll give you five now and five when you come to my house."

"Okay. It's a deal. Five now and the other five tomorrow. Hey, I know if I go with you now, I'll never live to see tomorrow."

"Now, now, son. What makes you think such a thing? What can I say? Do you want your money or not?"

The Judge handed Steven a brown bag that was in his jacket pocket. As soon as Steven took the bag, Malone and O'Malley were out of their seats and ready to handcuff the Judge and his wife. "Hey, what do you think you're doing? Do you know who we are?"

"We sure do. And you are both under arrest for conspiracy to murder your son, Dan Cramson." O'Malley read each their Miranda rights. When they frisked the Judge, they removed a 45 from his side holster. "What's this?"

"I'm a judge, and I need to protect myself and my wife."

"Of course, you do. And that's why you and your wife can have protection wherever you go. Funny, you didn't think you needed it here." The judge blustered, and both he and his wife argued that they had no grounds to arrest them. They gave Steven a death glare warning him that if he took a plea, that would implicate them and he would regret it.

With the arrests made, and both Jude and Steven willing to testify against the Judge and his wife, both Mark and Lacey could breathe a little easier. Jude confessed that he aided when he agreed to deliver Dan's equipment to Steven. He admitted that it was greed and jealousy that enticed him to agree to such a diabolical scheme. Although he did not want to see the demise of his stepbrother, two-hundred and fifty

CHAPTER 19

thousand was hard to pass up. However, his conscience bothered him the night before, and that's why he slipped Dan the note. He thought Dan would call or at least question it. Even with the confession, he was charged with being an accomplice to murder. Steven was charged with second degree murder and attempted murder. The Cramsons were both charged with conspiracy to murder in the first degree. They were all held without bail.

Judge Cramson and his wife hired Steven to tamper with his gear. He realized what a fool he was to agree to do this for a mere fifteen grand. He had no idea that the Judge would get two million in an insurance policy.

The Judge's huge gambling debt was exposed. He had convinced his wife that since she could not tolerate Lacey as a daughter-in-law, they could benefit by cashing in the policy. When they were told that Lacey was pregnant with their grandchild, the future heir to their two million, they knew Dan and Lacey had to be eliminated. Sadly, they had basically disinherited their son when he had married Lacey. How shallow, all because Dan's wife was not one of the elites they thought their son should have married. The only way they would collect was to not have Dan or Lacey in the way. Their heir would be their granddaughter, she would collect the two million. Since they would be her legal guardians, the money would be theirs.

It was a relief to walk out of the courthouse knowing justice had been served. Their trial and sentencing would not be for some time. They only hoped it would be sooner rather than later.

Lacey's heart went out to Dan's brother, Jude. She wanted to forgive him and give him a second chance. He would come out of prison and have no one. It would be some time before she could face the Cramsons knowing how much they hated her. Lacey knew in her heart she would have to forgive them for her own good.

CHAPTER 20

One more week of Lamaze. and they would be done. The final class was on feeding and bathing your newborn. The bathing and burping were a breeze but nursing was a little embarrassing. Lacey could tell that Mark was doing all he could not to watch the instructor or the video. His red face gave him away. This had to be as awkward for him as it was for her. She tried her best to make light of it. When the class was over, they were extremely proud to receive their certificate of completion.

Lacey had one more doctor's appointment before her due date. Mark seemed just as excited as she was. Now that the Cramsons were no longer a threat, Lacey thought a lot about Mark staying with her and the baby. She knew she loved him with all her heart. She had found peace in letting go of Dan. Oh, she would always love Dan—there would always be a special place in her heart for him. She realized that God designed the heart big enough to love again. However, she had no idea how Mark felt about her. She would not force him to stay with her. She had to let him go to find the woman God intended for him. She did not know how she would go on without him—but go on she must.

"Well, my dear. Your little girl is ready to enter the world. It won't be long now. I want you to call as soon as you feel the time is right. When you notice the contractions get closer together, make your way to the hospital. We don't want you to be miserable. Daddy, will you be available to take your wife to the hospital? How far away do you work?"

"I'm about a half hour away. I thought about working from home if labor starts early. I think we are both anxious to greet our little girl." Mark gave Lacey a wink that melted her heart a little bit more. She wondered when she should broach the subject of him staying after the baby is born.

After the doctor's appointment, it became a habit to go out for lunch. The car ride was extremely quiet; neither talking much at all. When they sat down at their table, Mark reached across to hold Lacey's hand while he prayed. As soon as he ended, he looked up at Lacey only to see her watery eyes. "We have to talk." They each said in unison. That at least brought a chuckle from Lacey. Mark stared into her eyes, "do you want to go first, or should I?"

"Mark, I don't know if I can talk right now. Why don't you go first?"

"Okay. Lacey, I have to just get this out." He was so nervous—he thought his heart would stop. He took a deep breath. "Lacey, I can't leave you. I know if you don't want me to stay, I'll understand. I agreed to be with you until the baby was born. However, now … I can't just walk away, not when I feel the way I do about you." His hands were sweating. "I can stay out of your way, and only care and protect you and our baby. I know that it may be impossible for you to love me. But I can't leave … I can't just walk a—" *Man, am I rambling or what?*

Lacey reached across the table and grabbed his hand in hers. "Mark, that's exactly what I wanted to talk about. I don't want you to leave. Mark, I love you with all my heart. How could I not? If you will have me, I want to be your wife … completely."

"What? Did you say you love me?" her head bobbed up and down. "Lacey, I have loved you for so long." Mark felt himself beginning to tremble all over. He would never cry but he sure felt like he would.

"You have? How long?"

He sure felt sheepish admitting he loved her from the time she walked into their office. "Well, I guess it's best to say I had deep feelings for you." *Okay, I might as well admit it.* "Lacey, ever since that first day you walked into the office, I was sure I fell in love with you— your

CHAPTER 20

warm smile, your beautiful green eyes; you had a way of brightening up the entire office."

"Why didn't you say something? I was so hoping you would have asked me out but you never did."

"I couldn't at the time. I was caring for my mom and sister. Then, when Jessie went missing, it was all I could do to make sure she was all right. Dan knew I really liked you and asked if it would be okay with me if he asked you out. I had no hold on you, Lacey. He was my best friend; I couldn't tell him no. I had to admit that it took me a while to see you only as a friend and Dan's wife. I really had to pray about my feelings for you." Lacey sat there stunned to hear his confession. She knew more than ever she could trust him with her heart and their baby girl.

Their ride home from the restaurant was way different than to the restaurant. Lacey reached her hand out to Mark so he could hold it on their drive. If the console wasn't in the way, she would have sat as close to him as possible.

Before they went to bed, Lacey asked Mark if he wanted to sleep with her; to her shock, he said no. "I want to wait until we have a wedding with my family and our friends from church. What do you say?" Lacey agreed; she could not believe how thoughtful he continued to be. But tonight, before they each went to their separate rooms, Mark wrapped her in his arms and said goodnight with a warm, passionate kiss, stirring an unquenchable hunger for him. She was sure her toes curled. "Sweetheart, this is going to be torture. At least I can hold you and kiss you like a man should his wife." He kissed her one more time. She kissed him back with just as much passion. When he fell into bed, he thought his heart would burst right out of his chest—that's when he felt tears slide down his cheeks. *Could this possibly be happening to me? God, thank you so much. I certainly don't deserve someone like Lacey but I'm so thankful."*

The scene wasn't much different in Lacey's room. *How did I get to be so lucky to have a good man like Mark?* She realized luck had nothing to do with it, but it was definitely God's plan for her life. A plan she could never had imagined.

Chapter 21

Mark woke with a start as Lacey stood above him. "I think it's time, Mark." She was dressed in her sweats and a large top. He shot up, almost hitting Lacey in the jaw.

"Oh, honey, why didn't you wake me sooner?" He began to fumble for his pants, wallet, keys, and phone. "There, I think I have everything. Let's go."

Lacey began to giggle. "Mark, you don't have everything." She pointed to his bare feet. "I think you're forgetting shoes and socks."

"Oh, gee. I'm okay. Um, where do I keep my socks?" He looked at Lacey who had gotten a pair out of his drawer. "Do I have time to put them on? Maybe I should just wear my shoes without socks."

"Mark, you have plenty of time to put both your socks and shoes on. You need to get my bag by the bed. Oh, no, oh, no!"

"Lacey, what's wrong?" She was looking at the floor.

"My water broke. I'm sure I'm ready." Mark grabbed her bag and then helped her down the stairs. "Mark, I think I can walk by myself." He wasn't even listening to her as he held onto her making their way to the garage. Mark opened the garage door, got in the car and began to pull out of the garage. Lacey stood there with her mouth agape. Mark pulled back into the garage, got out, and helped Lacey into the car.

"Sorry about that. I'm good. Really, I'm good." He carefully backed out of the garage, almost forgetting to close the door. Before it closed all the way, he saw her bag left on the garage floor. He opened the door again and jumped out of the car to retrieve her bag. When he got back in the car, his heart was pounding so hard it felt like he had been on one of his morning runs. His forehead and palms were sweating.

"Mark, do you want me to drive?"

"No. Of course not. I'm fine. I can do this."

He didn't know how they made it to the hospital, but they did. He got a wheelchair and an attendant for his wife and followed them in. He was thankful they had valet service at this hospital as he handed the valet his keys. *Maybe now I can breathe a little easier. No. That's not happening.* His wife was whisked away immediately, leaving him to fill out the necessary forms. His hands shook so badly that the kind admittance employee asked if he wanted her to fill them out. She very gently asked him all the pertinent questions.

Mark was directed to the elevators, taking him to the 5th floor. "There's a waiting room for dads and as soon as your wife is in her room, they will come and get you."

"Okay, thanks." He had no idea how he made it to the 5th floor, but he did. He stopped at the information desk and was directed to the waiting room. He began pacing around the room. He waited for an hour, no, two hours at least, for the nurse to come for him. *I can't believe it's taking so long. What is wrong?* When he looked at his watch, it was only 15 minutes. *Well, it felt like a long time.* Finally, a nurse came and directed him to Lacey's room. At least for now she looked a lot calmer than he felt. "Hey, sweetheart, how's it going?"

Her eyes had been closed but as soon as she heard Mark's voice they opened. She greeted him with a huge smile. "I'm good for now. My contractions are about eight minutes apart." With that said, she gave out a moan and grabbed Mark's hand. "That one was a little harder." Her smile returned. The nurse came in and explained everything that was going to take place. His job sounded simple ... so far; hold her hand, rub her back, give her ice chips, and basically encourage her. He could handle it, if only his heart would start beating normal.

CHAPTER 21

"Mark, are you okay? You seem awfully jittery. Did you have more coffee?"

"No, Lacey, I'm fine. It isn't every day that a guy becomes a father. I just want to make sure I get everything right."

"I'm not worried. I know you will. You're going to be an amazing daddy." Lacey saw the sheen in his eyes; more important she saw the love and devotion for her.

After three painful but glorious hours, they heard the sweetest words from Dr. McDonald—"Happy birthday, Hope Elizabeth."

Mark gave Lacey a wink that melted her heart, and then he brushed a gentle kiss on her lips. "Congratulations, Mommy."

They had picked out their little girl's name over a week ago. When Mark shared a verse in the Bible with Lacey, I Peter 1:3, "Praise be to the God and Father of our Lord Jesus Christ! In his great mercy he has given us new birth into a living hope through the resurrection of Jesus Christ from the dead," her eyes lit up.

"Mark, can we name our baby Hope Elizabeth? Elizabeth was my mom's name."

"Oh, Sweetheart, absolutely. I love it. You and our baby are heaven's gift to me."

The nurse laid a precious pink bundle in Lacey's arms. "Mark, she's perfect."

"Just like her mom."

CHAPTER 22

It was three weeks since Hope was born. Mark continued to be a big help by working from home as much as possible. Only when he had to be in court did he leave her alone with the baby and his mom. Mark's mother, Agnes, had come from Florida to help as well. Lacey certainly felt like she was being doted on. In three more weeks, she would be getting married ... again; this time in their church with family and friends. Agnes was thrilled that she would see her son married in church—this had always been her dream for her son. She loved Lacey and continued to be amazed at how God had worked it all out. It was evident that Lacey loved her son with all her heart.

Agnes brought the mail in for Lacey and set it on the kitchen counter. Baby congratulation cards were still being sent to them. The women at church had given Lacey a beautiful baby shower the week before Hope was born. She had never felt more loved since her mom and dad had passed away. It saddened her that she would have no family to attend her wedding, but so very thankful for Mark's family. Lacey sat at the table with Agnes having coffee when she began to open the mail. "Mom, I can't believe all the cards we have been receiving." Agnes was thrilled when Lacey asked if she could call her mom.

She opened one envelope that was a letter, not a card. Tears began to appear in Lacey's eyes. "Oh, honey, what's wrong?"

"Mom, nothing's wrong. This is a letter from someone who says she thinks I'm her sister." She handed Agnes the letter. "I don't know what to think of it. She says she is five years younger than me. She wrote that our mother put me up for adoption when she gave birth to me at sixteen. Five years later she was born. We have the same mom and dad. My mom married my father four years after I was born. Could this all be true?"

"She also writes that you have two younger brothers as well."

"I think Mark should check this out. How would she even know where I live? I don't want to get my hopes up that I have my own family." Lacey began to tell Agnes her story and how she knew she had been adopted as an infant but never knew her biological mother.

"I think Mark would be able to verify if what this woman says is true. He should be home from court soon."

"Yes, he texted me that he was on his way home." Agnes saw her swipe a few tears that had escaped her water-filled eyes.

Agnes reached across the table to take hold of Lacey's hand. "Oh, honey, I'm sure it comes as quite a shock to have family you never even knew existed."

She gave a nod. "I don't want to get my hopes up. What if it's some cruel prank?"

"What's a cruel prank?" Mark had walked into the kitchen overhearing only that part of the conversation.

Agnes handed Mark the letter. Not taking a seat he began to read. Lacey nibbled on her bottom lip wondering what he was thinking. When he looked down, he saw the tears in his wife's eyes. He wrapped his arms around Lacey, reassuring her that he would look into it.

"Mark, how would anyone even know how to reach me?"

"I think I have an idea. When we went through the ordeal with the Cramsons, we did have our picture in the paper."

"I never thought of that."

"I'll still investigate it. Will you let me handle this?" as he held up the letter. Mark squeezed Lacey's hand.

"Of course, I will." Just then the baby monitor let out a soft gurgling sound. "It sounds like Hope is waking up from her nap."

CHAPTER 22

"You sit, you too, mom, I'll get her." The gesture warmed Lacey's heart to see how involved Mark was with their daughter.

"He certainly loves his little girl."

"Yes, he does, Mom. She has him wrapped around her little finger already."

Chapter 23

Two days later and Mark was convinced the letter was legitimate. He had set up an appointment with Lacey's sister, Madeline. He arranged to meet her at a Starbucks in Arlington. When she walked in, he was shocked at how much she looked like Lacey; you simply could not mistake them for sisters. "Wow, you and Lacey look so much alike!"

"When I saw her photo in the paper, I thought I was looking at myself. I showed the article to my mom; that was super hard for her. I had no idea that I had an older sister."

"My mom told me her story. She got pregnant and had a baby girl when she was sixteen. Her parents, my grandparents, insisted she put the baby up for adoption. When she was nineteen, she married my dad. I guess my grandparents did not approve of my dad, but at nineteen, they couldn't stop them."

"How does your mom feel now about you contacting your sister?"

"Honestly, she's afraid Lacey would not want to meet her. I saw the pain in her eyes when I showed her the newspaper picture. I'm sure it's something she has regretted all her life. I also have two younger brothers. Of course, they know nothing about having another sister. I think I'll leave that up to my mom or dad to tell them."

Mark sat there in disbelief, silently praying that her mother would be able to forgive herself for the past. "Lacey and I will be getting married in three weeks."

"Wait. What did you just say? I thought she was already married to you."

"Yes, we are married but it's kind of complicated. I'll let her explain it to you."

They set up a meeting when they could meet her mom. He was in awe that the man her mom married was her biological father—what were those chances? Mark could not wait to tell Lacey.

Lacey was shocked that both her biological parents were married to each other; for all these years. She was amazed that they lived in Fort Worth, not that many miles away. She stood fidgeting with her hands and biting her lower lip. "Mark, I'm so nervous. What if this is wrong? I'm probably messing up their perfect family."

"Lacey, honey, I'm sure they want to meet you. Your sister was especially hopeful. Now relax. They'll be here any moment." No sooner did Lacey take a seat on the couch, the doorbell rang. She looked up at her husband and gave him a nod.

Mark greeted Lacey's mother, Cheryl, and her father, William. Her sister, Madeline, and her two brothers, Dean and Danny, followed. Lacey looked somewhat overwhelmed when they all entered. She stood to greet her new family. Madeline, with tears in her eyes, immediately put her arms around Lacey giving her a warm embrace. "I can't believe after all this time I get to meet my sister. The sister I never knew I had." She giggled as she said this.

When her mother reached out to her, the dam broke. Her mother, with tears streaming down her face, opened her arms. "Can you forgive me?" All Lacey could do was nod and run into her mother's arms.

There wasn't a dry eye among them. Even the two brothers sniffled. Her father, William, stood totally choked up as he wiped the tears that had escaped.

Lacey saw where her green eyes came from; her dad had the same eyes. They sat on the couch with Lacey in between—each holding her hand. They told Lacey and Mark their story of young love and heartache when Cheryl was forced to give her baby up for adoption. "That was the hardest thing I ever had to do. My parents wouldn't allow William

CHAPTER 23

to even see me once I told them I was pregnant. He never got to see his baby girl. You were so beautiful. However, right after your birth, you were given to your adoptive parents. My parents never knew that I continued to write to William. He joined the military at 18 and when he got out at 22, we married." Cheryl looked at her husband with such love. "I couldn't believe he still wanted me after what my parents did to him."

"Hey, I loved you at 15 and never stopped. I loved my baby girl even if I never had the chance to see her. Now, I can't believe I'm seeing her for the first time." He looked Lacey in the eyes. "And you, my dear, are absolutely beautiful."

Lacey felt herself blush. "Thank you." Lacey had not noticed that Mark had left the room. When he returned, he was holding their baby girl. Lacey beamed at Mark as he placed Hope in her arms. "I want you to meet your granddaughter, Hope Elizabeth." She looked at her mother and asked if she would like to hold her. It wasn't long before Hope had been passed to each of them. "Boys, this is your niece." She was surprised that even they were willing to hold her.

Agnes came into the living room with a tray of homemade cookies and banana bread. She got their beverage orders and went back into the kitchen to get the coffee and sodas. Mark followed his mom into the kitchen. "Mom, that went well. I'm so happy for Lacey."

"Yes, they seem like good people. That's quite a story I heard them tell. I couldn't help but overhear them. Mark, Lacey has such a big heart to embrace them the way she has."

"Mom, ever since her parents died when she was nineteen, she has longed for a family. As much as I have told her our family is now her family, I think deep down it's just not the same as connecting with your own flesh and blood. Madeline said her mom was afraid that Lacey would hate her for what she did."

CHAPTER 24

The church was packed with friends and family. Lacey wore the same beautiful light green linen dress she wore at the courthouse. Looking back on that day, it was a real wedding as far as she was concerned. This wedding was for family and friends. She was amazed she could still fit into her dress six weeks after giving birth. Her hair was pulled back in an elegant chignon entwined with lily of the valley. Her bouquet was a beautiful arrangement of pink roses, astrimaria, and lily of the valley. A cascade of pearls wove through and flowed out from the bouquet.

She walked out of the bride's room with her mom and Agnes. One of the ushers escorted the two moms to the front, one on either side of the isle. Her father stepped beside her offering her his arm. He looked dashing in his tux. He whispered in her ear. "I can't believe this is happening. I'm walking my baby girl down the aisle." Lacey squeezed his arm and whispered to him. "I love you, daddy." He was sure he would lose it right then and there.

After her two bridesmaids walked to the front, Lacey and her newly-found-father began their walk, arm in arm. Lacey's heart began to pound when she looked up to see her handsome husband waiting for her, holding their baby girl. When they got to the front of the church, he gave her a wink and handed Hope to Agnes.

As Mark stood with Lacey, holding tightly to her hands, all he could think of was how close he came to losing her and their baby. Yes, he knew Dan would always be Hope's biological father; he could never take that away from him, but he would raise Hope as his own. His heart would always ache for the loss of his best friend.

Mark was thankful for Pastor James who officiated; Judge Larsen, his good friend who had married them in his chambers the first time; and his brother-in-law, Jason. Yes, he felt so blessed to have these solid men standing with him as he renewed his commitment to his wife. They wrote their own vows; this time he told her how much he loved and cherished her and their baby girl. Lacey's vow was filled with devotion and a promise to love him from this day forward. Mark beamed when Pastor James said you may kiss your bride. It was not a light peck on the cheek but a kiss that spoke of an undying love.

The reception was held at the country club where Mark had been a member for several years. He insisted on a live band which Lacey thought way too extravagant. Lacey could not believe the warmth and affection that encompassed the entire celebration. Having the entire Edwards family in attendance was truly a blessing. The love from this family flowed from each of them. It was obvious it made an impression on her family.

When it came time for the bride's dance, Mark wrapped her like a cocoon in his embrace. She had to admit that this wedding meant more to her than her marriage with Dan; now she knew a God who loved her unconditionally, and she had married into a family that put God first. That made all the difference in the world.

That night, as they placed their sleeping baby girl in her crib, Lacey felt Mark's strong arms wrap around her. The warmth of his embrace was comforting. "Well, Mrs. Hamilton, will you go to bed with me tonight?"

Lacey turned to look at Mark with hunger in her eyes. "I've been waiting for you to ask me." Finally, they would be a real married couple in every way possible. Lacey turned to look at their baby girl. "Mark, we never talked about any more children but I would love to give our daughter a baby brother or sister."

"How about we give her both?"

The End

Thank you for reading *Heaven's Hope*. I trust you enjoyed reading it as much as I enjoyed writing it. I know this is not quite a third book to the Edwards Brothers, however, I consider it to be part of a series as many of the characters are the same.

I hope you got a small glimpse of God's unconditional and sacrificial love for each of us as you read Heaven's Hope. God pursues us with a fierce love as He patiently waits for us to open our hearts to Him. He wants the best for us. John 3:1 says, "How great is the love the Father has lavished on us, that we should be called children of God!" You may be a Lacey and have never personally responded to the love and grace Jesus freely offers or have never acknowledged you're a sinner and in need of a Savior. You can do that right now in the quiet, wherever you may be. As it says in Colossians 2:13, "When you were dead in your sins, God made you alive with Christ. He forgave us all our sins." He came to make dead people alive.

Blessings,
Kiki